*Praise for The Laird's Christmas Kiss:*

"*The Laird's Christmas Kiss* was a delightful romance that I didn't want to put down. I loved Elspeth and Brody... This story was exactly what I wanted to read at the holidays." **Kathy's Review Corner**

"With familiar characters from the previous book and Anna Campbell's witty dialogue, this was one of those books I just couldn't put down!" **5 stars Rose Is Reading**

"I loved this, it was a great quick read which hit all the historical high notes for me. It had the dashing, devilishly handsome Laird and a shy but witty take-no-nonsense female lead who has always had a thing for the Laird." **Beyond the Pages**

"A real holiday treat." **Rakes and Rascals**

"The story was a very charming little read and I highly enjoyed it and I recommend it to any historical romance fan that likes a little holiday in their novels." **5 stars Amazon Review**

"*The Laird's Christmas Kiss* is both light, yet serious, as it showcases family dynamics, insecurities, friendships, and misunderstandings. But most of all, it's a warm and entertaining holiday romance with a satisfying happy ever after." **Roses Are Blue**

"I'm not sure I can come up with enough synonyms to describe Ms Campbell's stories. They are always delightful, the characters somewhat cheeky, and have interesting twists. I'm enjoying the Laird's series and this story was no exception." *Australian Romance Readers Association*

"I am a huge fan of Anna Campbell short stories. She is a talented writer who always packs in lots of heart into her pages. I always know that everything is going to work out so I enjoy the ride and let Anna spin her tale." **Top Pick.** *Night Owl Reviews*

"I absolutely loved this novella, it was well written, paced nicely, gave glimpses of Fergus and Marina's HEA, had witty banter, steamy love scenes, great secondary characters and a sigh worthy declaration." **5 stars** *Amazon Review*

"An outstanding love story to enjoy while you curl up in front of the fireplace with a hot mug of cocoa." **5 stars** *The Reading Wench*

"Another beautiful Scottish historical Christmas holiday romance book by Anna Campbell. It is the perfect type of story about love, faith, confidence and trust. About a forgotten lass and an overconfident lad and soon the tables turn and the opposite happens. Yet it's Christmastime a time for magic and the power of love. Anything is possible at Christmas! I absolutely loved this story and the multidimensional characters kept me on my toes. Another riveting story that I couldn't put down!" **5 stars** *Celtic Barb's Tartan Book Reviews*

"Delicious." **Susanne Bellamy, Bestselling Author**

"A wonderful Christmas story." 5 stars *GoodReads Review*

# ALSO BY ANNA CAMPBELL

Claiming the Courtesan

Untouched

Tempt the Devil

Captive of Sin

My Reckless Surrender

Midnight's Wild Passion

## The Sons of Sin Series:

Seven Nights in a Rogue's Bed

Days of Rakes and Roses

A Rake's Midnight Kiss

What a Duke Dares

A Scoundrel by Moonlight

Three Proposals and a Scandal

## The Dashing Widows Series:

The Seduction of Lord Stone

Tempting Mr. Townsend

Winning Lord West

Pursuing Lord Pascal

Charming Sir Charles

Catching Captain Nash

Lord Garson's Bride

**The Lairds Most Likely Series:**

The Laird's Willful Lass

The Laird's Christmas Kiss

The Highlander's Lost Lady

The Highlander's Defiant Captive

The Highlander's Christmas Quest

The Highlander's English Bride

The Highlander's Forbidden Mistress

The Highlander's Christmas Countess

The Highlander's Rescued Maiden

The Highlander's Christmas Lassie

**A Scandal in Mayfair Series:**

One Wicked Wish

Two Secret Sins

Three Times Tempted

**Christmas Stories:**

The Winter Wife

Her Christmas Earl

A Pirate for Christmas

Mistletoe and the Major

A Match Made in Mistletoe

The Christmas Stranger

His Christmas Cinderella (in the anthology A Grosvenor Square Christmas)

**Other Books:**

These Haunted Hearts

Stranded with the Scottish Earl

# The Laird's Christmas Kiss

The Lairds Most Likely Book 2

ANNA CAMPBELL

To my dear friend Christine Wells who always
inspires me!

# CHAPTER ONE

*Achnasheen Castle, Western Highlands of
Scotland, December 1818*

Elspeth Douglas loved many things. Her family; her horse Chester; her home in beautiful Glen Lyon; daffodils; shortbread; Walter Scott's novels; rainy days curled up on the sofa in front of the fire.

And Brody Girvan, Laird of Invermackie.

Nearly everything on that list loved her back—although perhaps not the luscious, buttery shortbread. She'd needed to let her favorite frock out an extra inch for this Christmas house party. But Brody Girvan, to her infinite regret, didn't know she was alive.

Now she sat in front of her dressing table mirror in her pretty bedroom in Achnasheen Castle and acknowledged the bitter truth. When it came to love, she'd set her sights too high. The dashing Laird of Invermackie was never going to view her as anything but a distant acquaintance, one of a crowd, nobody special.

Accepting this unpalatable fact ripped her heart to shreds because, ever since her first encounter with charming, disreputable Brody Girvan five years ago, she'd been under his spell. She hadn't been quite sixteen. That was an impressionable age for a girl, a time when she was prone to infatuations with unattainable objects of desire.

Elspeth, with her dreamy, romantic soul, was more prone than most to powerful adolescent passions. Brody's wild, dark eyes, and wild, dark curls, and penchant for riding the most unmanageable horse in the stables, were sure to set her innocent heart fluttering.

Of course, back then, when she was a spotty, plump, bookish fifteen and her beloved was a worldly twenty, she'd barely entered his consciousness. He hadn't noticed her mooning around Glen Lyon all summer, frantic for a mere glimpse of him.

Most girls left their youthful fancies behind as they matured. But while Elspeth had grown out of her spots, and during this last year, her figure had gained some shape—despite the shortbread's evil machinations—her heart had never wavered. It was Brody's from the moment she saw him take a reputedly unrideable stallion over a high fence, then race across the hills with a careless élan that stole her breath away.

To her regret, in the years since that momentous day, Brody's heart hadn't shifted either. He remained happy to flirt with any attractive woman in sight, and get up to unknown wickedness in Edinburgh, and ignore the quiet girl who worshiped him from afar.

Now Elspeth surveyed her unimpressive reflection and decided she really couldn't blame her idol for failing to fall at her feet and declare his love. The Laird of Invermackie was everything exciting.

While she...wasn't.

Elspeth was the cuckoo in a family of peacocks. Or rather the humble sparrow. Cuckoos made their presence felt more than she ever had.

Her mother was one of the two famous Macgrath sisters, notable beauties who had dazzled London society before making brilliant marriages to rich Scotsmen. Elspeth's mother had since become a powerful political hostess, and her influence had helped her husband rise high in the War Office. On the way, she'd borne five children: Elspeth's older sisters Grace, Charity and Prudence, then the longed-for heir, Hamish. Eight years later, her mother's "afterthought" arrived.

Elspeth had been an afterthought in her family ever since.

Most of the time, she didn't mind. Life as the sole quiet member of her noisy, brilliant, opinionated, physically splendid family had its compensations. It allowed her to sit back and observe. It let her do just what she wished, because nobody paid her a scrap of attention.

But when it came to attracting the man she wanted, her self-effacement was a complete disaster.

Discontentedly she counted off her mediocre physical attributes. Brown eyes. Brown hair. Unremarkable features. She wasn't hideous, her face was quite pleasant, but as memorable as a potato. She sighed and bit her lip, and told herself she'd cried enough over Brody Girvan. Tears had never done her an ounce of good.

She mostly lived at Hamish's home in Glen Lyon near Oban. Her brother had scorned the idea of following his father into civil service and spent his time being frightfully Scottish on his rich estates when he wasn't dazzling London's intellectual establishment with his astronomical discoveries. A couple of times a year, he and his cousin Diarmid got together with their great friend Fergus Mackinnon, Laird of Achnasheen. Various family members often turned up to share the fun.

Brody Girvan was Fergus's cousin. While he didn't always appear at social gatherings, he was present often enough to remind Elspeth that no other man would ever match him.

Much good that did her either.

This year, there were changes in the air. The Christmas party was more exclusive than usual, and for the first time, Fergus and his bride, the famous artist, hosted the seasonal festivities at Achnasheen. This afternoon, Brody had arrived with Diarmid, and Elspeth had a sick feeling that when he greeted her in the crowded great hall, he'd struggled to remember her name.

Now she met pensive brown eyes in the mirror. She'd had enough of feeling rejected and disregarded and boring. Things were due to change for her, too. She wasn't going to be in love anymore. She was twenty years old, and it was time to grow up and forget silly infatuations.

No more broken heart. She was a mature woman, and she'd act like one.

So, take that, Brody Girvan.

She would embrace the fact that she was dull and drab. No longer would she eat her heart out for what she could never have. A new, free life started today, and may she be hauled through thistles in her nightie before she devoted another moment to yearning after handsome young men who wasted their best years in idleness and dissipation.

To prove she'd claimed the higher ground, the mature woman made a face and poked her tongue out at her uninspiring image.

Brody Girvan, Laird of Invermackie, was altogether a dashing fellow. Or at least that was what people told him.

But as he sauntered down from his bedroom at Achnasheen, crossed the medieval great hall with its seasonal decorations of holly and pine, and approached the breakfast room, he harboured the unwelcome suspicion that he wasn't quite as dashing as he wanted people to think.

On his first night back in his cousin's home, he'd stayed up with Hamish and Diarmid, drinking far too much of Fergus's excellent whisky. It was good seeing his friends, but he greeted the morning with a headache and the grim knowledge that he frittered away his life and youth on pleasures that began to pall.

For months, this feeling had been growing on him. At first, he'd given it the cut direct. After all, what else could any man want but plenty of reckless women to warm his bed and the freedom to pursue whatever vices beckoned?

But his lurking dissatisfaction hadn't taken its dismissal in good spirit. It had pursued him, like bailiffs harrying a laddie who hadn't paid his tailor's bill. Over recent months, its clamor had risen to the point where ignoring it took more effort than anything else in his hedonistic, useless life.

Good God, was that really how he'd describe his gilded existence?

He refused to admit that it was. But last night and too many nights before that, he'd sat up late carousing with cronies, while wishing he'd gone to bed with a good book instead.

What a shameful admission for a rake to make.

There was no arguing that today he hadn't slept until noon as was his habit, but instead was up at the unheard-of hour of eight. The devil knew why. Nobody else seemed eager to face the snowy morning. The castle was as quiet as the grave, and as was the norm in Scotland in December, outside it was howling a gale. In dreich weather like this, even a bloody parson could find an excuse to sleep late.

Grumpily Brody slouched into the breakfast room. He caught the smell of bacon and kippers and whatever the hell other instruments of torture his cousin Fergus had set out in the name of sustenance. His stomach rebelled. He swallowed sour bile and told himself that under no circumstances would he start his day by casting up his accounts.

Anyway, he placed the blame in the wrong quarter. He should credit the menu to that black-eyed, half-Italian witch Fergus had married a little over a year ago.

Except that wasn't fair. Brody liked Marina, Fergus's unconventional bride. Although he couldn't help noting that his restlessness with a perfectly pleasant life dated from seeing his once self-sufficient cousin in thrall to a woman. And as happy as a Scotsman in a haggis factory.

Blast it, at this rate, Brody might start contemplating marriage, too.

At first, he thought the breakfast room was empty—which suited his curmudgeonly humor. Then he saw a girl watching him from the shadowy corner beside the buffet.

"This room is as dark as a deuced coalmine in Hades," he growled, before he reminded himself that he was supposed to be a gentleman, with at least a distant acquaintance with manners.

"And good morning to you, too, Brody," the girl said in a flat tone, carrying her plate across to the table. She chose a seat that offered her a view across the snowy lawns to the loch.

It was the Douglas chit, the youngest sister, the quiet one. The only brunette in a family of blazing, golden blonds.

"I'm sorry. I've got a devil of a head," he said, before wondering if confiding the night's excesses to a well-born virgin was quite the thing either.

"Then by all means, don't feel you have to make conversation," she said, with more of the faint sourness that had tinged her greeting.

Shocked, Brody paused on his way to the buffet, seeking not food but the coffee pot. The lassie spoke to him as if he didn't deserve her attention. When he appeared, girls always brightened up and played with their hair and went all giggly and arch.

He frowned across at this wee brown wren. She looked anything but giggly or arch. In fact, she showed no pleasure in his company at all.

How bizarre.

The lassie began to eat her porridge with dogged dedication, as if he wasn't there. Surprise thundered through him, stole his breath. Good Lord, she was ignoring him. Girls never ignored him.

He shouldn't be piqued. But he was.

Feeling grumpier than ever, Brody prowled across to the coffee pot and raised it in her direction, wondering if he'd catch her observing him under her lashes. She wasn't. Instead, she was staring out the French doors at the discouraging weather. With

Christmas only four days away, today promised snow all through the festive season.

"Would ye like some coffee?" he asked, to interrupt whatever profound, non-Brody-related thoughts she enjoyed.

She turned her head and inspected him the way she'd look at a slug on her salad. "My name's Elspeth."

He became seriously annoyed now. Too much whisky must make a man short-tempered. Which was odd, because as a rule, he was the most easygoing of laddies, even after a night of kicking his heels up.

*You're easygoing only because you always get your own way,* a nasty wee voice sniped in his mind. That nasty wee voice had moved in at the same time as his general dissatisfaction. He'd spent a year wishing it to Jericho, but so far it remained entrenched, and inclined to offer an opinion when least welcome.

"I know that," Brody responded with a hint of impatience. "You're Hamish's wee sister."

Elspeth's lips tightened. Had he said something wrong?

"I wasn't sure you remembered me."

"Of course I remember you. Our families get together two or three times a year. I'd need my head fixed, if I didn't remember you." He waved the coffee pot at her, only just missing spilling it. "Now, Elspeth, Miss Douglas, Hamish's wee sister, would ye like some coffee?"

"No, thank you," she said, with a politeness that shouldn't irk, even if it did.

Like the rest of her family, she spoke with an English accent that turned the insincere courtesy even frostier. The Douglases were as Scots as Brody was, but they'd grown up in London, where the late

Laird of Glen Lyon had been someone important in the War Office during the conflict with France.

When Brody poured his coffee, he slopped it in the saucer. That annoyed him, too. Generally he was brimming with savoir faire.

He swallowed the first cup so fast, he burned his mouth. Trust Fergus to make sure his guests got hot coffee. Still feeling disgruntled, he poured another cup and crossed to take the chair opposite Elspeth.

He drank this cup with more care, using the opportunity to take stock of his companion. Family gatherings tended to be chaotic, and crowded, and full of large personalities jostling for space. While he'd always known this girl was there, he'd never paid much attention to her.

She was surprisingly pleasant to look at, now he took the time to find out. A touch of the Madonna, with her oval face and deep brown hair drawn back in a simple knot. Creamy skin, and a nice, generous figure. A bonny bosom, too, although that mold-green dress with its collar fastened up to her chin did nothing to show off her assets.

Brody wasn't in favour of overly skinny girls. He liked a soft armful of a lassie to keep him warm. If a laddie got young Miss Douglas into his bed, she'd offer him a good, comfortable landing.

Which was not a thought he should have about his friend's sister.

When her mouth flattened under his inspection, he saw she was aware of his scrutiny and didn't like it. Apart from that luscious bosom, her mouth was her best feature. Full and expressive, and offering an intriguing hint of unawakened passion.

With a glare, she set down her spoon. "It's rude to stare."

In his experience, girls liked him looking at them. Actively encouraged it, in fact. It seemed he needed to file Elspeth Douglas under a different category from the females he knew.

"I was just thinking that I've known ye for years, yet this must be the first time we've spoken alone."

Large brown eyes turned larger with surprise and focused on him. A brown deep enough to drown in. Eyes brilliant with intelligence and surrounded with thick, dark lashes. He found himself wondering if her eyes might be her best feature after all.

"We're...we're not exactly speaking." Her voice was unsteady.

"I apologize for my lack of address." Two cups of coffee made him feel almost human. He managed to scrape up a smile. "I'm not used to being up at this ungodly hour."

"No," she said, without smiling back. "I've never seen you at breakfast before."

"Perhaps I'll get up early more often, now I ken what charming company awaits me."

It was the kind of gallant remark he made without thinking and which always elicited a flurry of feminine fluttering from the recipient. Elspeth merely sent him an unimpressed glance and rose to serve herself some bacon and scrambled eggs.

He must be feeling better. The sight of the food on her plate made him hungry instead of ill.

"Do ye ride, Elspeth?" he asked, after he'd got himself some breakfast. "Fergus and Marina have suggested going out on the hills, if the weather doesn't worsen."

He didn't know why he tried to make conversation. Every time he spoke, the girl stiffened up as if she feared he set out to lure her into some wickedness. Perhaps she'd heard about his reputation as a Lothario.

Perhaps? Of course she had. Brody was under no illusion about the way the members of his circle gossiped about each other.

Was she afraid that he meant to flirt with her? That wasn't his impression. Instead he felt like she considered him a damned nuisance, and she'd rather he went away.

The surprise was that he was in no mood to cooperate. The world was full of pliable-minded lassies. Why on earth was he so curious about this wee tabby kitten all of a sudden?

She took her time examining his question for hidden meanings, then responded warily. "Yes, I ride."

He smiled again. Again she didn't smile back. "Perhaps we can ride together."

And wondered why the image flooding his mind depicted riding of a very different sort. She wasn't at all his style, if one disregarded that voluptuous, yet too modestly covered figure. He tended to chase much more obvious—and obviously available—quarry.

*Which is why you're bored stiff with your conquests,* said the horrid, persistent voice.

*Go away,* he said back, without any hope that it would listen.

Another small delay, then the girl said, "Perhaps."

He was gearing up to push for something more definite—and enthusiastic—when a maid came in with fresh coffee. He bent his head and began to eat, surprised at how famished he was.

By the time they were alone again, he had another cup of coffee on the table before him, while Elspeth sipped her tea. "How long are ye staying at

Achnasheen?" he asked, not sure why he persevered, but persevering anyway.

"Until after New Year," she said.

He'd intended to leave after Boxing Day, but now he changed his mind. "Me, too."

"That's longer than usual," she said in a neutral voice.

This was the first indication that she'd paid him any attention over the years. Pleased, he said, "I'm looking forward to seeing more of Marina and Fergus, given this is the first Christmas they're hosting here."

"Yes, it's meant a change, hasn't it?" At last, she sounded almost friendly.

He was about to follow up on the thaw, when Diarmid, blast him, came bouncing in. His friend was awash in good spirits, which seemed dashed unfair, given the amount of bad spirits he'd imbibed in Brody's company last night.

"Elspeth, I should have known you'd beat me to breakfast. How did ye sleep? I slept like a baby." The tall, handsome, charming bastard came forward and kissed the girl's cheek with a familiarity Brody couldn't lay claim to. After all, the two were cousins, whereas he was a mere family friend. "Hope this snow stops before too long. The plan is to go riding later."

For the first time that morning, she smiled. "Good morning, Diarmid."

Her face expressed fondness, with a touch of the humor she'd signally failed to share with Brody. Diarmid beamed back, then turned to Brody. "Good morning, my lad. Thought you'd be nursing a headache."

"Not at all," Brody said coldly, wishing his friend to Hades.

"I suppose that's one benefit of all that licentious living," Diarmid said, before he toddled off to pile a plate high with food.

Brody wanted to tell his friend to shut his blasted mouth. A man's entertainments were his own business. More, he cursed Diarmid for interrupting an encounter that showed signs of heating up from near freezing.

The moment Elspeth had smiled—not at him, damn it—he recognized why he'd decided to put off his departure. The next few days offered intriguing possibilities, and he was just the man to take advantage of them.

# CHAPTER TWO

The weather soured as the day progressed, preventing the promised riding expedition. Elspeth was grateful. Now she'd decided to abandon her foolish penchant for Brody Girvan, it seemed cruel to be thrust into his company. Not that she believed he'd meant a word of what he said about riding with her if they went out.

She'd had years of observing him as closely as only an adolescent girl observed the object of her affections. He liked to flirt with any pretty woman in his vicinity. This morning at breakfast, pretty women had been thin on the ground, so he'd made do with her.

She didn't mind. Or not too much. After all, a girl who was the afterthought in her own family had no delusions about her ability to hold a raffish young man's attention.

Thank goodness, Diarmid had come in and put a stop to the awkwardness. Nor had Brody's sudden interest turned her head. Once she might have taken his invitation as a sign of awakening attraction. But after last night's bracing conversation with herself, she accepted that he'd never pursue her in any serious way.

Now, after dinner, the guests relaxed in the greenery-bedecked great hall. Huge fires burned in the two hearths, warming the air, defying the inhospitable conditions outside.

From where she sat on a sofa, Elspeth surveyed the gathering. Hamish, Fergus, her mother, and her sister Charity played cards in one corner. Prudence thumped out Christmas carols on the piano, her husband Charles standing behind her and turning the pages. Charity's husband Donald read a book near the fire. Diarmid sat at a desk under the windows, writing letters. After a day of running around the castle, shrieking with excitement, Elspeth's nieces and nephews were asleep upstairs.

While Elspeth didn't mean to pay him an ounce of special attention, she couldn't help looking for Brody. With a glass of whisky in one hand, he stood alone at one of the high gothic windows and stared out at the falling snow.

Elspeth supposed these family entertainments must strike him as abysmally dull, after the dissipated life he led in Edinburgh and London. She was surprised he planned to stay so long at Achnasheen. His habit was to make an appearance, then leave after Boxing Day. Perhaps he changed his plans this year because the festivities took place at his cousin's castle. Before this, they'd all celebrated Christmas on Hamish's estate, with her mother as hostess, and all three of her older sisters and their families joining them.

Elspeth reminded herself that she was no longer interested in Brody Girvan's doings, and she went back to her novel, although for the life of her she couldn't remember a single word of the story.

"May I join you, Elspeth?" Marina, her hostess, asked from beside the sofa.

Elspeth glanced up with a smile. She didn't know Fergus's wife well, but what she knew of her, she liked. "Of course."

"If you're enjoying your book, I'll happily sit here without talking. I've never hosted a big house party before. *Per dio,* it's much harder work than being a guest."

"I'm sure."

As she sat, Marina's instinctive grace made Elspeth green with envy. Lucky Marina, to be so tall and slender. A short little pudding like her could never aspire to that languid elegance.

"Is it a good book?" Marina slid a pencil and a small sketchpad from her pocket and opened it to a blank page.

Elspeth gave a huff of self-derisive amusement. "I have no idea. I've been woolgathering for the last hour."

"Cozy winter evenings encourage that." Marina began to sketch a vivid picture of the card players, using only a few, economical lines. Fascinated, Elspeth watched as swift strokes of the pencil captured Fergus in all his lean, auburn-haired magnificence, then dark, handsome Diarmid.

"You're lucky being able to do that."

Marina smiled absently and with a sweep of her pencil delineated the fall of Elspeth's mother's extravagant bronze velvet gown. "Yes, I am."

"Fergus tells me you're having an exhibition in Edinburgh in April. That must be exciting."

"It is. Landscapes, of course. I only do portraits as a hobby. I hope you'll come."

"I'd love to." She paused and decided that now she'd grown up, she needed to be brave and say what she thought. "Especially if you tell me where you buy your clothes. I love what you wear."

She might envy the other woman's grace and talent, but she'd kill for the panache to wear that crimson silk evening gown. It turned black-haired Marina into a column of living flame.

"*Grazie.*" Marina's hand fell still, resting the pencil on the half-finished drawing. "Are you saying you'd like a new look?"

Elspeth cast a disparaging glance at her blue merino frock. "I am."

"Your mother is always dressed *à la mode.* Doesn't she help you to choose your clothes?"

"She has other fish to fry. Specifically fish of either the Tory or the Liberal variety."

Marina smiled at the small joke about Lady Glen Lyon's political activities. "But you're her daughter."

Elspeth's smile was fond but wry. "By the time I came along, Mamma was way past any interest in bringing up another girl. My arrival was a surprise—Hamish is eight years older than I am. With the rest of the family so handsome, Mamma decided I didn't give her enough to work with."

Marina frowned, rolling the pencil between her fingers. "You do yourself an injustice."

Elspeth shook her head. "I don't think so, although I know I must sound horridly sorry for myself."

"*Un poco.*" Marina's lips twitched. "A little perhaps. But I'll forgive you."

Elspeth smiled back, liking this unusual woman more and more. "Thank you."

Marina was regarding her with an assessing gaze. "You know, if you stopped being so self-effacing, you could give your family some competition."

Elspeth's laugh was dismissive. "How kind you are."

"Not at all. I'm looking at you the way an artist does. With the rest of the Douglases, the eye goes straight to that golden fairness and the height. And *ovviamente,* they are all proud like lions and know they're beautiful. Look at your mamma over there. She's still a great beauty, even though no longer young. She's used to the world paying her homage, and she takes it as her due. You, on the other hand, are inclined to cling to the sidelines and watch what's happening, as if you have no right to join in."

Elspeth winced. "That artist's eye can be quite ruthless, can't it?"

"Sometimes I'm a little too frank for politeness." The hand holding the pencil made an apologetic gesture. "I'm sure it's because I'm half-Italian. I'm sorry if I've upset you."

"No, you're right." Hadn't Elspeth said something similar to herself last night in her bedroom, when she'd forsworn all longing for a certain Brody Girvan?

Who had turned his gaze away from the window and toward the corner where she and Marina sat. Not that she paid him any heed. That wasn't what the new Elspeth Douglas did.

To her mortification, her hostess noted the way her attention strayed in Brody's direction. "*Cielo,* these Highlanders are spectacular men. When I first saw the Mackinnon, I was sure there couldn't be a man in the world to match him for handsomeness. Then I met your brother, who is golden and powerful like Apollo. And the dark, intriguing Diarmid, with his looks in the style of the famous Lord Byron."

Elspeth rolled her eyes. "You still think Fergus is the handsomest. You two positively glow when you're together."

Marina's smugness was charming. "Perhaps I'm biased." She nodded in Brody's direction. "Although your young Laird of Invermackie vies with his cousin, when it comes to dashing looks."

Despite having relinquished all thought of Brody as anything more than a family friend, her cheeks heated to fire. "He's not *my* Laird of Invermackie."

Marina appeared puzzled. "Then why does he keep looking over here?"

Elspeth shot a fleeting glance toward Brody, who did indeed look spectacular tonight. All the gentlemen sported kilts, and she couldn't help thinking Brody wore his clan's green and blue plaid with particular distinction. In standard evening dress, he was dangerously attractive but still connected to civilization. In traditional Highland garb, he looked untamed and elemental, at home in this ancient castle with its history of warfare and romance. Even for a girl who was a mere family friend, the sight was enough to steal every ounce of her breath.

He caught her eye upon him and tilted an enquiring black brow. She thought her blush couldn't get any hotter. It turned out it could. Flustered, she turned back to find Marina watching the interplay with a knowing expression that Elspeth didn't like.

"He must be looking at you, Marina." Not that Elspeth could blame him. Marina was so dark and dramatic. She doubted Brody had serious designs on his cousin's wife—the gossip she'd heard kept him just a whisker on the right side of honor—but nobody could fault a man for admiring a pretty woman.

"Oh, my dear," Marina said in a wondering tone. Elspeth braced to hear more nonsense about him noticing her at last, but Marina fell silent.

Elspeth looked down at the book clasped between her hands, then chanced another glance at Brody. He'd gone back to gazing out the window, and the slump of his shoulders hinted at discontentment.

That struck her as curious. Whenever they met, he bristled with animal good spirits. It seemed odd he hadn't joined in the cards either, or invited the other gentlemen to play billiards.

Perhaps this intimate Christmas gathering left him at a loose end. When Hamish hosted the party, the entire Douglas family descended on Glen Lyon, and for a few days life turned into a rabble of aged relatives and boisterous children and puppies. Now the only dogs were Fergus's collies Brecon and Macushla, and the ranks of visiting children had thinned to four of her nieces and nephews.

Perhaps Brody still suffered from last night's excesses.

And perhaps it was time for someone who no longer pined for his affections to think about something else.

Elspeth met Marina's perceptive gaze. She prepared for some sly comment about her interest in Brody, but Fergus's wife just inspected her as if she was a landscape suitable for painting.

"You know, you have great potential. You have good skin and lovely eyes, but the colors you choose don't do anything for you." She paused, giving Elspeth a chance to bask in surprised pleasure at hearing that she had "lovely" eyes. "And if you don't mind me saying this, you dress far too young. You're a *bella ragazza*, but nobody would know it under the schoolgirl frocks."

Elspeth bit her lip in chagrin. "I never spend much time thinking about what I wear."

Marina gave a huff of impatience. "Then it's high time you did. How can you hope to catch the eye of a handsome laird, if you look like you're still doing your Latin homework and holding your governess's hand to cross the road?"

She shifted uncomfortably and began to wish she'd stuck to her book instead of invited this conversation. "I told you—Brody is my brother's friend."

Marina arched her eyebrows. "I didn't say the laird had to be Brody."

As if he heard his name mentioned, he turned his head in their direction once more. Elspeth lowered her voice to a mutter. "I'm not the sort of girl he finds appealing. He likes loose women."

Marina's smile was worldly. "Of course he does, but perhaps if you venture out from behind the pages of your book, he might like you even better."

"I like to read."

"So do I. But you're hiding your light under a bushel, *bella*. Or under Walter Scott's newest romance, anyway. It's time you stepped out to shine."

Blindly Elspeth stared into space, for once too churned up to notice Brody Girvan. Could she shine? Over the years, her mother and sisters had made half-hearted attempts to bring her out of her shell, but it had always been easier to retreat and go back to being a turtle.

Last night, something in her had changed. She'd relinquished futile childhood dreams and decided to grow up. Perhaps part of growing up meant making the best of her meager attractions.

"I've upset you." Marina's lips flattened in distress. "I'm sorry."

Startled, Elspeth looked at this striking woman who was so frank—and so helpful. "Not at all. It's embarrassing how right you are. I appreciate that you're brave enough to tell me."

Marina's eyes brightened. "*Brava, ragazza.* If you're serious about wanting to change your style, come upstairs with me tomorrow after breakfast, and we'll see what we can do."

Excitement filled Elspeth. With Marina's help, perhaps she was on the way to a new version of herself. She'd long been unhappy with the original edition. "I'd love that. Thank you."

# CHAPTER THREE

"Why the deuce are ye brooding over here on your own, laddie?" Diarmid asked, jolting Brody out of his weighty reverie. "Has some wench in Edinburgh turned you down? You're like a damned lost dog this week."

In truth, he wasn't quite as moody as he'd been first thing this morning. Or at any time in the last year or so. Standing at the window, he could watch his sparrow girl without making her unduly uncomfortable. She always pokered up when she knew he was looking at her.

How on earth had he missed that Elspeth Douglas was so bonny? She dressed like a frump, and she was reluctant to put herself forward, but he was considered a connoisseur of feminine beauty. He should have noticed her before this.

Nor was she in his usual style. But the sweetness in her expression drew him more powerfully than his previous lovers' overt attractions ever had. In fact, he was becoming deuced sick of overt attractions. Perhaps it was time he sought something a little more subtle.

"Brody? Good God, man. It's worse than I thought. You're lost in your own world."

"Very amusing." Without any great interest, he turned to Diarmid. "I haven't exactly noticed ye being the life of the party either."

Diarmid shrugged, unoffended. Despite his dark, romantic looks, he was the most even-tempered man Brody knew. They'd been friends for years, since not long after Fergus, Diarmid and Hamish met as boys. But Hamish's cousin remained in many ways a mystery. "Nobody expects me to dazzle the company. You, however, have a reputation as an unregenerate rascal to uphold."

Brody bit back a testy reply. What Diarmid said was true. Brody was accounted a man with an eye for the ladies. Did that mean he was nothing more? Not long ago, he might have relished the idea that the world considered him a rakish fellow. Now he wondered if this meant he was too shallow to enjoy the long-term happiness his cousin had found with Marina.

"Oh, stow it, Diarmid. Can't a laddie spend a wee bit of time in thought, without his friends making fun of him?"

Diarmid's black brows arched in mockery. "Thought, is it? And here was I mistaken in believing that ye set your sights on Hamish's sister."

Damn, he'd hoped his sudden and uncharacteristic interest in Elspeth Douglas had gone unnoticed. That was the thing about Diarmid—you could never guess what the bastard was thinking. And the worst of it was he was always thinking.

"They're both married," he said, hoping to deflect attention from his sparrow.

Diarmid's smile scorned the weak evasion. "Elspeth's not, and you've been eyeing her off all night."

He shrugged. "At least she's no' committed elsewhere."

"She's also far too good for a libertine like ye."

Shocked and resentful, far more than he could justify, given his history, he glared at the man he called a friend. "What the devil are ye trying to say?"

Diarmid remained unruffled. "She's nice, and she doesnae deserve to have her heart broken by a careless philanderer."

Brody drew himself up to his full height, which didn't mean much, seeing both he and Diarmid were around six feet two. He narrowed his eyes and spoke in a low, dangerous voice. "Are ye saying you've got rights there, Mactavish?"

He couldn't help remembering that Elspeth hadn't been overly pleased to see him at breakfast, whereas she'd lit up like a bloody lighthouse when Diarmid appeared.

"Are ye saying you want rights of your own, Girvan?"

"You're her blasted cousin," he spat, even as he felt sick at the idea of that lovely girl in Diarmid's arms, cousin or not. It was a surprise to realize that he didn't want Elspeth Douglas in anyone's arms but his.

"Aye, which is why I have to keep her out of the clutches of womanizing scoundrels," snapped the usually good-natured Diarmid.

"What on earth is going on?" Fergus barked. Brody had been so involved in the spat, he hadn't noticed that the game of cards had finished and his cousin approached them. "It's supposed to be the season of goodwill, yet ye two look ready to kill each other."

The tension flowed out of Diarmid as if it had never existed, while Brody remained sickly aware that the fellow hadn't answered the question about his interest in Elspeth. He was also aware that beneath the jealousy he had no right to feel, he was hurt that Diarmid harbored such a low opinion of him. He'd always liked and respected the other man, but it seemed the esteem wasn't mutual.

"Just a wee philosophical disagreement," Diarmid said, and Brody envied how fast his friend regained his customary composure. He still felt ready to explode like gunpowder at the first provocation.

"Take it outside."

"It's bloody snowing," Brody protested.

"I know." Evil dripped from Fergus's smile. "It might cool ye both off."

Marina came up and slid her arm through Fergus's. Brody wondered if he was right to suspect that she and Elspeth had been talking about him. He hoped so. "*Tesoro*, shall we have some dancing? Charles has offered to play, to make equal numbers of men and women."

Fergus smiled down at his wife, a headstrong, independent woman who was the complete opposite of every other lassie he'd ever chased in his thirty-odd years. The warmth in his gray eyes made Brody's notoriety seem cheaper than ever. "As long as I get to dance with ye, *mo chridhe*, I thoroughly approve."

"*Bene.* We might have a couple of waltzes and quadrilles, and perhaps a reel or two."

She clapped her hands and soon had everyone lined up facing one another. Charles launched into a jaunty tune on the pianoforte, and the dancing began. Brody ended up opposite Charity. He didn't mind. One of the pleasures of these country dances was that a man got to partner all the ladies in turn.

Elspeth was three couples down, with Hamish. If she'd been dancing with that condescending bastard Diarmid, Brody might have been less sanguine.

It still seemed to take forever for the ladies to work down the line, but at last he reached out to catch Elspeth's hand as they and the next couple formed a star and circled. When his large hand closed over hers, her coffee-dark eyes flashed in his direction. Perhaps she reacted to the contact like he did. Her touch set his heart crashing like a great drum and shot sizzling heat up his arm.

Did she feel the same attraction? The flare of awareness had been too brief for him to be sure it even existed. Those sumptuous eyelashes fluttered down, and she retreated into mystery once more.

Because of the odd number of pairs, he and Elspeth stood out for a turn, while the others continued with the dance. He kept hold of her hand, although there was no strict requirement that he should. Her fingers fluttered in his, but she didn't pull away.

"I believe we're meant to make conversation while we wait," he prompted with gentle mockery.

Another flicker of those remarkable eyes in his direction. Every time she focused on him, he had the uncomfortable sensation that she saw past his polished outer self to his soul. Did she, like Diarmid, consider him a worthless fribble? Or did she find some redeeming qualities? He fervently hoped she did.

"Where are you going when you leave Achnasheen?" she asked.

*Wherever you are.*

But he couldn't say that. Not yet, anyway. "Back to Invermackie. I'm overdue to visit."

When she licked those full lips, another bolt of heat jolted him. "Not...not Edinburgh?"

He shook his head and avoided Diarmid's glare as the other man swung Hamish's mother around in the dance. "I'm a wee bit weary of Edinburgh."

Elspeth was watching him again with that serious expression. He was unused to girls who didn't try to flirt with him. He wasn't quite sure how he should act.

"Perhaps London might offer better entertainment."

"I doubt it." His lips tightened. "It's all more of the same, isn't it?"

She shook her head. "I wouldn't know. You must be so very jaded. Edinburgh and London sound exciting to me. I lead a quiet life in Glen Lyon."

The hint of wistfulness in her voice touched him. He squeezed her hand and only just stopped himself kissing her. And wouldn't that put Diarmid's kilt in a twist? "I'd love to show ye those places one day, Elspeth."

She cast him a startled glance, but he was saved from having to explain his remark because it was their turn to rejoin the dancers. As was the way, another partner swept her off. Brody found himself facing Marina, the woman who had sparked his seething discontent.

What a pity he liked her so much.

As he swung her around in the center of the square then promenaded down the line, she smiled. "You like her."

Despite his years of debauchery in Edinburgh's salons, Brody found himself blushing like a schoolboy. Of course he bloody liked Elspeth. Still, a man had his pride to keep up.

"Who?" he said with a disingenuousness that failed to convince his cousin's wife. It didn't even convince him.

"The cook's cat, of course." Marina said with asperity. "Who do you think I mean? I begin to think that I've been wrong to underestimate your good taste."

He frowned. "What is that supposed to mean?"

Marina arched her eyebrows. "You know exactly what I mean."

To his regret, he did. Elspeth was as far removed from his usual inamoratas as gold from iron pyrites. "She likes Diarmid," he said gloomily.

Marina scanned down the line to where Diarmid swung Elspeth. "*Si*, she does. *Cielo*, he's such a handsome devil."

Ladies had a weakness for the dark, brooding type. It was a pose Brody, too, had adopted with notable success.

The dance's energetic movements put pink in Elspeth's cheeks. She didn't look at all the shy wee wren he'd always thought her. She laughed at something that slimy bugger Diarmid said. She never bloody laughed at anything Brody said to her.

Jealousy stabbed him, more powerful because it was an unfamiliar emotion. "You're not making me feel any better," he said sourly.

He mightn't make Elspeth laugh, but no question, he amused Marina. He wished that counted. "Cheer up. Perhaps she'll start to notice your good qualities."

"I'm not sure I have any," he said before he could stop himself.

Brilliant black eyes shot him a critical glance. "*Per pietà*, you'll have to dig some up, if you want to woo that lovely girl. Your wicked Edinburgh ways aren't going to win you any battles in this fight."

What was the point of arguing? She was right. As they took their place at the head of the line, he shot her a straight look. "What were ye and Elspeth talking about on the sofa?"

"When you couldn't take your eyes off her?"

He ignored that. "Were ye talking about me?"

Marina rolled her eyes. "No, we weren't. We were talking about dresses."

"Oh," he said, unable to hide his disappointment.

"Chin up, Brody. If you've grown up enough to notice Elspeth, you've grown up enough to work out how to catch her."

Before he could object to a remark which annoyed him on so many levels he didn't know where to start, they changed partners again, and he was back facing Charity.

# CHAPTER FOUR

y the time Charles started to play a waltz, Elspeth had almost recovered from that astonishing conversation with Brody. Then her heart, barely back to beating at a normal rate, started to race again when the man she refused to love anymore strolled toward her on those long, powerful legs. He had almost reached her, and the breath jammed in her throat, and the room receded down a long tunnel, and...

"May I have this dance, sis?"

She blinked to bring the whirling scene back into focus. Hamish stood in front of her with his hand outstretched. She was nodding and rising from her chair, before the great weight of disappointment could crush her. Because a woman who didn't love Brody Girvan had no right to feel devastated when she missed the chance to twirl around the room in his arms.

Brody paused a few feet away and invited Prudence to be his partner.

Elspeth made herself smile at Hamish. "Of course."

Marina's impromptu ball proved a great success. By the time Donald sat at the pianoforte so

Charles could dance with his wife, Elspeth had waltzed with every male in the room except Brody.

At the end of a cotillion, she saw him approaching, arm in arm with Marina, who looked flushed and happy. A pang of something that might have been jealousy—if she still cared for Brody— pricked Elspeth, before she noticed Fergus striding toward his wife. It was plain that all Marina's rosy joy stemmed from the prospect of dancing with the man she loved.

"I've done my duty, *mo chridhe*," Fergus said. "May I dance with my wife now?"

Marina laughed and shot him a flirtatious glance from under her thick black eyelashes. "If you ask nicely, *caro*."

"Nothing as poor spirited as that." Fergus flashed her a smile. "I'm going to sweep you into my arms and out onto the dance floor, whether ye agree or not."

Lucky Marina, Elspeth couldn't help thinking. Brody stepped away from his hostess, as she took her husband's hand. "I can't wait."

True to his word, Fergus whirled her out into the dance, leaving Elspeth alone with Brody. Slowly she raised her eyes to meet his and despite everything, she couldn't stifle a thrill at the glittering look of triumph she discovered there.

"I've done my duty, too. Now I want to dance with ye."

Out of the corner of her eye, she saw Diarmid marching toward her with a determined expression. Quickly she stretched her hand out to Brody. "I'd be delighted."

"I'm pleased to hear it." His smile was no less piratical than Fergus's.

The breath jammed in her throat at the magnificent sight of this man with his face creased in pleasure. When he caught her hand in a ruthless grip, anticipation rippled right to her toes in their blue satin dancing slippers.

She couldn't contain another thrill as he slid one hard hand around her waist. They began to move with the lilting music. Diarmid had turned aside and was now dancing with her mother.

Elspeth was afraid she might stumble, now they waltzed together. In the past, the mere mention of Brody's name was enough to make her butter-fingered and as clumsy as a newborn filly. Deciding she didn't love him did wonders for her poise. Her feet fell into the pattern of the waltz as naturally as if she'd been born to dance with the Laird of Invermackie.

The room was large and the party was small, leaving Elspeth and Brody plenty of space to move without worrying about the other couples. The music swirling around them was the sweetest melody she'd ever heard. Heaven help her, this was like flying among the stars.

Once she realized she wasn't going to disgrace herself on the dance floor, she met his green gaze. He was studying her with a dedicated concentration that made her heart crash into her ribs with forbidden excitement.

"We've never waltzed before," he said, staring at her as if she was the prettiest girl in the world.

What a flirt he was. He just couldn't help himself. Now she'd gained some distance from her adolescent yearnings, it was easy to see how he'd talked all those ladies into sin.

"The Douglas family parties have always been too staid for such a scandalous new dance." Thank goodness, she even managed to put a few words together without sounding like a tongue-tied ninny. Not being in love was good for her. She should have tried it long ago. "If people had waltzed at one of Hamish's Christmas celebrations, Aunt Agatha would have had a fit. She doesn't much approve of dancing at the best of times."

The heat from Brody's touch seemed to seep through her whole body. When his large hand shifted to bring her closer, she caught the drift of his scent over the fresh sap of the pine branches decorating the room. Sandalwood soap. Young, healthy male. Something intriguing and spicy that she suspected might belong just to him.

Sharing his scent was breathtakingly intimate, although a few inches still separated them and kept the dance—almost—proper. Her silly heart started to turn somersaults, even as she gave it a stern lecture about how it should behave with a mere acquaintance.

"Good God, then she'd have a heart attack if she could see all this unbridled license tonight," Brody said drily. "People in each other's arms? Disgusting!"

"I've always been terrified of her. She's wont to lecture me on propriety."

"Then to the devil with the old besom."

Elspeth cast him an uncertain look. Brody couldn't be hinting that he'd like to lure her into misbehaving. Heavens above, he'd never even looked at her before tonight, and she was well aware that she wasn't a girl a rake would find of interest.

She retreated to a neutral statement. "Marina is going to ring in a lot of changes, I think."

"God bless Marina." When he smiled down at Elspeth, her heart performed a few more giddy acrobatics. She couldn't help it, and she refused to apologize for a feminine reaction that meant nothing beyond the enjoyment of the moment. When such a handsome man exercised his attractions, any lady would feel a flutter or two.

"I always imagined Fergus would marry someone meek and obedient. She's such a lovely surprise."

Brody performed a turn that made her head spin. By the time she caught her breath, the couple of inches between them had shrunk to a tiny gap that would horrify Aunt Agatha. Elspeth made a half-hearted attempt to establish a greater distance, but that firm grip at her waist wouldn't budge.

"She's not the only lovely surprise."

This time, even a woman determined to cling to good sense couldn't mistake his meaning. She sent him a repressive glance. "Brody, don't waste your time flirting with me. I'm frightfully dull."

He laughed, and she saw Diarmid shoot them a disapproving look. Then she caught Marina's eye. Marina didn't look disapproving at all.

Brody's sensual lips lifted in a sardonic curl. "I'm no' wasting my time, you strange and enchanting lassie."

For a moment, the room vanished, and all she saw was that dark, striking face with its brilliant green eyes and commanding blade of a nose. Then she remembered that she'd vowed to be sensible when it came to this man. "You're trying to turn my head."

He arched one black eyebrow. "Am I succeeding?"

"No," she said, although even now, she wasn't sure about that. "There must be better targets for all this charm."

He was still smiling down at her as if he really was enchanted. "You think I'm charming?"

This onslaught of masculine interest was all too heady for her. And unfair. Not to mention a little cruel. Because while Elspeth might have banished her ludicrous adolescent *tendre* for him, she wasn't immune to his appeal. Yet every minute proved that she'd aimed way above her touch when she'd set her sights on him.

Resentment sneaked out to color her response. "Does it matter what I think, when you're so convinced yourself?"

He looked startled and for a moment, she caught a hint of what might be injured feelings. Then his eyes sharpened in a way that sent a chill of disquiet rippling down her spine. "There's more to ye than meets the eye, isn't there, Elspeth?"

"I hope so," she retorted.

"I look forward to unwrapping the layers."

It seemed she possessed a wanton imagination. Who would have guessed? While she knew he couldn't mean those words in a literal sense, she couldn't help picturing him removing her clothes, and...

Elspeth stumbled, and his grip on her waist tightened. She hoped to heaven she wasn't blushing, but when she met knowing dark eyes, she was sure she was.

"Watch your step," he murmured.

"Oh, I will," she said, finding her balance again.

She waited for another mocking response, but instead he led her through a series of dizzying turns that set her heart rushing. It was almost worse when he didn't talk. The silence left her too conscious of that tall, elegant body moving close to hers. He looked marvelous in the kilt, as rugged and untamed as this beautiful land where he belonged.

Because the dance was informal, they weren't wearing gloves as they would at a society ball. With her hand resting in his, she couldn't ignore his warmth and strength. The very air conspired against her. Every breath she took was tinged with the tangy essence of Brody. It was a good thing she'd decided to outgrow her love for him, because if she hadn't, she'd soon go quite daft.

"What are ye thinking about?" he asked softly.

"The scenery," she said, which was true, if not the whole truth.

A brief huff of amusement escaped him. "That's a shame. When we dance, I want ye to think of me."

She shot him a critical stare. "You're flirting again."

He shrugged and swept her into another turn. "I can't help myself. Every time I do, ye look like a startled deer."

It was her turn to laugh, although with a hint of chagrin. "Given you couldn't remember my name this morning, you can't blame me for finding your behavior a little puzzling."

He didn't smile but subjected her to an assessing stare that had her blushing again, although she wasn't sure why. "Of course I remembered your name." He paused. "And if I've been guilty of overlooking you in the past, that's because you set out to be overlooked."

His perception surprised her. She'd always been in awe of his spectacular looks. Now she wondered if she'd misjudged the brain behind those cool green eyes. Fergus was clever. It wasn't beyond the realms of possibility that Brody was, too.

Was there a chance that she'd underestimated him, just as he'd underestimated her?

The waltz came to an end and saved her from having to respond to his last uncomfortable remark. Donald was closing the music and standing up from the piano. Marina and Fergus devoured one another with their eyes. The others stood around, talking and laughing.

Elspeth waited for Brody to lead her off the dance floor, but he kept his hand on her waist, anchoring her to the spot. "I suppose I should let ye go."

Drat. This time, she was sure she looked like a startled deer, much as she disliked the description. "It's bedtime."

He gave a mock groan. "I know."

She frowned. "You're being wicked again."

"Aye, I am." His smile was unrepentant. "Can I see ye tomorrow?"

She should move away, return to her mother, but some weak, female part of her liked the possessive weight of his hand on her waist. "Of course you'll see me tomorrow. It's not as if I'll get lost in the crowd. There are only eleven people in the party, if you don't count the children."

He was staring at her as if he'd like to eat her up. Almost like Fergus stared at his wife.

She shivered. Her romantic interest in Brody had been a young girl's ardent passion for an unattainable prince, essentially innocent. But today, something had changed between them. The attraction she felt—that any woman would feel, she assured herself—was much more adult.

She would no longer dream of Brody falling to his knees before her and declaring eternal devotion. Now she got to know him better, she realized that wasn't his style at all. Instead, she had an unwelcome inkling that tonight, her dreams would be full of his hands on her body and kisses that were hungry rather than worshipful.

"You ken what I mean," he said steadily.

Not altogether, but she had a clue. "Yes, you can see me tomorrow."

"I can't wait." He released her waist and before she had a chance to regret her promise, he caught her hand and brought it to his lips.

For a charged moment, she felt the heat of his mouth on her skin, then she was free. "Good night, sweet Elspeth. Dream of me."

Curse him, she had a horrid feeling she would. "Good night," she stammered, then turned with relief when her mother came up to her.

"Lady Glen Lyon," Brody said, bowing. "It's been a bonny evening."

"It has." Her mother spent a few moments sparkling at him before she turned toward the door, taking Elspeth's arm. "My, oh, my, that Brody Girvan is a fine-looking man."

"Yes, he is," Elspeth said, with difficulty keeping her voice steady. Her fingers still tingled after that brief kiss, and she surreptitiously opened and closed her hand behind the flare of her skirt.

"And how he does love to charm the ladies. I hope he's not finding this party too dull, where the only unattached females are a woman old enough to be his mother and a shy little mouse like you."

Just like that, the burgeoning happiness in Elspeth's heart shriveled to bitter absence. Her feet had felt lighter than air when she danced. Now they felt as if someone had strapped lead bars to her soles.

What a pathetic nitwit she was. Brody was making the best of a bad situation. How could she have missed that the pickings at Achnasheen were slim for a man who liked female attention?

All that burning focus on her had been a game. She was the only available woman. Or at least the only one at a susceptible age. Of course his interest wasn't genuine.

As if it would be.

When nasty reality set its claws into Elspeth, something in her revolted at always being belittled and disregarded. Brody had made a fool of her tonight, but he wouldn't find her so easy to ignore again.

Her mother might deride her meager attractions, but Marina said she had potential, and Marina was clever and perceptive. Be damned if Elspeth would ever let anyone call her a mouse again.

# CHAPTER FIVE

*E*lspeth's rebellious mood survived a restless night, which she spent telling herself that she deserved her humiliation. Hadn't she sworn that Brody Girvan would have no more power over her emotions? Yet the moment she met those glittering green eyes, she was as besotted as ever.

Never again.

So she managed to maintain a cool air when he joined her for breakfast. To her surprise, Diarmid wasn't much behind him. At the Christmas gatherings, both young men usually slept late, after sitting up to drink and play billiards, once everyone else went to bed.

That wasn't the only change. The air of constraint between Diarmid and Brody was new, too.

Brief curiosity sparked. What on earth was going on? Fergus, Hamish and Diarmid were the best of friends, legacy of a long ago escapade when Fergus rescued the two younger boys who had become lost in the mountains behind Achnasheen. Brody had always fitted into the group as if he belonged. But this morning, Elspeth couldn't mistake the lack of ease between her two companions.

Before she had a chance to winkle out the story, Marina swept into the morning room and hurried her away to the south tower.

"My goodness, you're on top of the world here, aren't you?" Elspeth said in amazement, as she stepped into the large and airy sitting room with windows facing in all four directions. She'd never been invited into the laird's private apartments at Achnasheen before. She paused to admire the view down to the sea, with the snow-capped Cuillins on Skye rising in the distance.

Marina laughed. "I often tell Fergus I only married him because no artist could resist the idea of living in such an extraordinarily beautiful location."

"He wouldn't believe you," Elspeth said with conviction.

Marina's striking features softened, so she looked extraordinarily beautiful herself. "No, he doesn't."

"Do you think you can do anything with me?" she asked, nervous hands twining at her waist.

"*Coraggio, cara.*" She left Elspeth standing in the middle of the floor and stood back to survey her with that intense attention, familiar after last night. "Are you sure you're ready for this? Once I've finished, you won't be lurking in the shadows anymore. I suspect sometimes the shadows are a welcoming place."

Elspeth recalled her mother describing her as a mouse, without a hint of spite, and Brody making do with her company because there was nobody better to flirt with. "You're right. The shadows are safe."

"Yes, they are." Marina watched her as if reading her thoughts.

"But they can become a prison," Elspeth said slowly. She raised her chin and squared her shoulders before she met Marina's penetrating black gaze. "I'm ready to be free."

"*Brava, ragazza.*" Marina smiled at her, then turned to open a door that led to a dressing room. "We have work to do, Sandra."

Marina's Italian maid, as stylish as her mistress in a gray ensemble banded with black velvet, emerged. She carried a pile of clothing which she tossed over the back of a pretty sofa, upholstered in flowered blue brocade.

"Those are all my dresses," Elspeth said in shock.

"I hope you don't mind." Marina made an apologetic gesture. "I thought first we'd see if any of your clothes are worth altering. Sandra worked for my *modiste* in Florence. When I decided to move to the wilds of Scotland, I invited her here to be my dresser. She's a genius with a needle."

"*Buongiorno, signorina,*" Sandra said, dipping into a graceful curtsy. "We make you *bellissima.*"

Elspeth had just enough Italian to understand and to cringe at the plan's impossibility. But she bit back any word of protest. The first step toward claiming self-assurance was acting like she already had it. She turned to Marina and spread her hands in bewilderment. "I thought you were just going to lend me a dress."

Marina smiled. "We're not at all in the same style, or I would."

"You're much slimmer than I am," Elspeth said, before she remembered that she meant to pretend to be confident. She spared a fleeting regret for all the shortbread she'd eaten over the years, to cheer herself up over her failure to win Brody Girvan.

"You have a magnificent figure. You're a true pocket Venus." Before Elspeth could grasp hold of such an extravagant—and astounding—compliment, Marina's tone turned practical. "Although only *il buon Dio* would know it under those schoolgirl frocks."

Elspeth shot the drab pile of dresses a doubtful look. In this lovely room and in comparison to the modish clothes the other women wore, her outfits looked duller than ever. "Do you think you can rescue any of them?"

"A snip here. A dart there. You'll be surprised. That's not all we're going to do. You need to change the shades you wear. *Basta,* no more browns and beiges and everything dull. No wonder you disappear into the wallpaper in dresses the color of mud. You should be in reds and blues and pinks and yellows. Strong shades to bring out your white skin and your sparkling eyes. I have some bolts of fabric from Milano and Firenze, that we can use for a few new gowns. But those won't be ready for tonight."

Amazed, daunted and touched in equal measure, Elspeth stared at Marina. She couldn't remember anyone taking this trouble over her before. "You're far too generous."

Marina laughed and rubbed her hands together with unmistakable enthusiasm. "I'll enjoy turning you into a beauty. It's an artistic project. And Sandra was becoming bored, with just me to fuss over." She turned to the maid with a volley of rapid Italian that Elspeth assumed was a translation of what they'd both just said.

Sandra surveyed Elspeth with that same steely focus Marina had devoted to her, then broke into a snaggle-toothed smile that added layers of charm to her bony features. She responded in the same language, and all Elspeth could make out were stray words like *bella* and *pronto.*

"*Si, si, certo,*" Marina said, and turned back to Elspeth. "Now, let's take off that ugly rag and see what we have to work with."

Before Elspeth could protest—although Marina was being so kind, what could she say?—Sandra started tugging at the hooks down the back of her dark brown merino. Elspeth clutched the sagging bodice to save her modesty. "It's not that bad, is it?"

Marina's smile was kind, too. "I'm afraid it is."

"Oh." Elspeth had come here because she wanted to change, but facing up to her frumpishness was no fun. She caught another glimpse of Marina's smile as Sandra hauled the dress over her head.

"Cheer up. Faint heart never won fair laird."

At least she could blame her blush on the fact that she now stood in the middle of the room, wearing nothing but her undergarments. "I told you—I'm not interested in Brody."

Marina's expression was suspiciously innocent when she circled Elspeth, as if she inspected a statue from every angle. "Brody Girvan isn't the only laird in the world."

Until now, for Elspeth, he might as well have been. She straightened her spine and told herself to stop being such a wet flannel. She'd already decided she wanted to make some changes. The way she looked was part of that. "No, he's not."

"*Brava.*"

Sandra stood back, her dark eyes never shifting from Elspeth. When she burst into more Italian, Marina looked thoughtful, before she moved closer to unpin Elspeth's tight arrangement of plaits.

"*Magnifico,*" Sandra said, as a wealth of dark brown hair tumbled down about Elspeth's shoulders. For once, no translation was needed.

"What beautiful hair you have," Marina said, lifting a thick hank of shining hair and letting it drift through her fingers. "Why on earth do you tie it away so tightly? *Per l'amor di Dio*, why on earth do you tie everything away so tightly?"

Overwhelmed with the confusing mixture of praise and criticism, Elspeth glanced down at herself. Her full breasts pushed wantonly against her white linen shift, and she felt stunted next to Marina and Sandra, both so tall and elegant. In a defensive pose, she wrapped her arms around her middle. "I'm not the right shape for the current fashion."

The hint of fondness in Marina's laugh removed any sting. "We can fix that."

"High waists make me look like a box."

Marina said something in Italian to Sandra, Elspeth guessed a translation of her self-deprecating remark. Sandra responded with what sounded like disagreement.

Still smiling, Marina turned back to Elspeth. "With your lovely bosom and small waist, the shape of thirty years ago would have been perfect for you."

"I told you," Elspeth said miserably, afraid that her mentor might decide she was a hopeless case after all.

Marina went back to studying her. Elspeth was getting used to it. "But with some lighter materials and someone who knows what she's doing like Sandra, we will succeed."

"In turning a sow's ear into a silk purse?" Elspeth asked before she could stop herself.

She expected Marina to laugh, but her hostess regarded her with a troubled frown. "Elspeth, you're a beautiful girl, and I can show you how to make the best of yourself, but the world won't believe that you've changed from a caterpillar into a butterfly until you believe it, too. I forbid you to say anything derogatory about yourself ever again."

Discomfited, Elspeth avoided those piercing dark eyes, as she struggled to come to terms with the idea of anyone calling her beautiful. Was it possible? When she'd accepted Marina's help, she'd harbored the modest hope that it might rescue her from fading into the background. Beautiful was an unimaginable step beyond that.

On the other hand, what did she have to lose?

"Yes, Marina," she mumbled.

"A little more gusto, *per favore, bella*." Marina carried a cheval mirror from the corner and set it before her.

In the reflection, Elspeth met uncertain brown eyes. This reminded her of the night before last, when she'd promised herself she was going to stop trailing around after Brody and take charge of her life. She angled her chin upward and surveyed the woman in the mirror.

"Yes, look, *cara,*" Marina said softly. "Look at yourself."

Marina said she could be beautiful. Marina was a stylish, sophisticated woman with an artist's eye. If she said that, perhaps it was true.

The girl reflected back was smaller than the two women ranged on either side of her. Out of her nun-like dress, even someone as self-critical as Elspeth saw that her curves weren't plumpness, but a graceful generosity of form. Her bosom rose above the corset, firm and round and white. Her waist was small, and her hips flared above shapely legs. Thick, glossy hair flowed around her face, adding a touch of mystery to features that she'd always believed irredeemably ordinary. Now she saw large, radiant eyes and a full-lipped mouth.

She didn't resemble her mother or her spectacular siblings. The dark coloring came from her father's side of the family. But nor did she look like a woman the world should ignore either. She looked...voluptuous.

A tentative smile lengthened her lips. Perhaps Marina was right, and there was something here to work with.

Approval lit Marina's black eyes, as she watched Elspeth's face brighten with new vitality. "*Si, cara, si.* Now you see what I see, and you know we'll succeed." She turned to Sandra with a torrent of liquid Italian, before she stepped back with a determined expression. "Let's get to work."

# CHAPTER SIX

As the day went on, Brody became restless and bored and out of sorts. The weather had worsened, confining everyone to the castle. He'd wandered the corridors looking for Elspeth, but despite her promise last night, she proved elusive. He'd seen her at breakfast—which made another early morning worthwhile—but Diarmid had arrived a few minutes after he did and proved a deterrent to flirting.

When he teased her last night, she'd been such a delightful mixture of confusion and gratification. He looked forward to teasing her again.

If he could ever bloody find her.

By the time everyone gathered to go into dinner, frustration had him ready to climb the walls. Where the devil was Elspeth hiding? Was she avoiding him? He'd swear she was as attracted to him as he was to her. He hadn't missed her shy pleasure in his attentions, or the way her eyes brightened when she saw him.

In a right royal sulk, he prowled into the crowded drawing room. Even before he entered, he heard the buzz of excited chatter. Once he stepped inside, he realized why. Without notice, Marina's father Ugolino had arrived from Italy.

And Ugolino hadn't shown up alone. At his side was a comfortably plump, middle-aged woman with a kind face and dark hair streaked with gray. Was it possible Ugolino had married again? He wouldn't bring a mistress here, not to a family party. A quick glance around the room told him that Elspeth wasn't downstairs yet. But everyone else was agog to hear what was afoot.

Brody might be preoccupied with his own selfish concerns, but even he understood that a new stepmother showing up unannounced would be a shock to Marina. He glanced across to see how she took the news.

"Such weather, *figlia mia*. Such weather." Ugolino and the lady must have arrived just that minute. He was taking off his snowy greatcoat and passing it to one of the servants. Beneath, his stout form was clad in the height of fashion. "Why couldn't you marry a man who lives in the south of France?"

"Nobody from the south of France asked me, Papa," Marina said, stepping up to hug her father. "You didn't tell us you were coming."

Ugolino shrugged with his usual careless charm. He'd spent years crisscrossing Italy, acting as his daughter's chaperone while she established her artistic career. Since her marriage, he'd become her agent in Florence, where he had great success selling Marina's paintings to rich young men doing the Grand Tour. "*Per pietà,* I was sitting at home by my fireside missing you, so I decided to give you a surprise."

"You've certainly done that," Fergus said on a grim note, coming forward to shake his father-in-law's hand. "Not least that you didnae arrive alone."

Ugolino looked sheepish and reached for the hand of the lady at his side. With the theatrical instinct natural to him, he waited until he had everyone's attention. "Friends and family, may I present my bride, Giulia?"

Marina's face went so still that she resembled one of her painted portraits. "Your wife?"

As Fergus caught Marina's hand, Ugolino brought his bride forward. "I was going to write, *dolcissima*, but then it seemed a better idea to bring Giulia to Scotland to meet you. She's heard all about you."

"Then she has the advantage over us," Fergus muttered. Following Ugolino's announcement, a thorny silence had descended.

"Giulia is the widow of the Conte di Massona, a nobleman from Verona. I made her acquaintance two months ago, when she and her son, the current count, called to buy one of your Highland landscapes. For both of us, it was the *coup de foudre*. We married three weeks ago. *Per carità*, at our age, there's no point waiting."

"I told you that this was no way to inform your family of our wedding, *caro*." Giulia sent her new husband a wry glance that expressed a mixture of affection and exasperation. "Before we saw the priest, we should have written to your daughter, or perhaps even waited until after she met me."

Ugolino raised Giulia's fingers to his lips and regarded her with glowing dark eyes. "But, *carissima*, I couldn't wait that long to make you mine."

With a surprise, Brody realized that the old charlatan was genuinely in love with his new wife. When he first heard the news, he'd wondered if the contessa's fortune and noble rank might explain her appeal.

Marina's shock faded, and she sounded almost like herself when she spoke. "Contessa, your English is excellent."

It was true. While Giulia spoke with a charming accent, her English was fluent and colloquial.

"*Grazie.* I had a Scottish governess when I grew up, and now with all the English milords traveling through Italy, I get lots of practice. With the hope of making a good impression on Ugolino's daughter, I've been working on my English during the journey, too."

"Have I done wrong?" Ugolino asked, eyeing his daughter with a humility that Brody suspected was at least partly manufactured.

"*Cielo*, of course not, Papa, but you're always full of surprises." Marina managed a smile, but Brody saw that she still reeled under the news. Nonetheless, she was a gallant creature, and she tried to make the best of the situation. She stepped forward and kissed her new stepmother on the cheek. "Welcome to the family, contessa. I hope you and my father will be very happy together."

The new Signora Lucchetti subjected Marina to a searching gaze, but what she saw must have reassured her. The warmth in her smile made her look years younger. "You're too kind. I hope that we'll be friends."

"I do, too," Marina said, and she sounded as if she meant it.

Ugolino smiled at his daughter with visible relief. "I want us all to have Christmas together like *una famiglia.*"

"Let me introduce you to everyone." Marina gestured toward Fergus, who looked unhappy with the situation. He was always fiercely protective of his wife. He'd be furious if her father's impulsive actions injuring her feelings.

While everyone else paid their respects to Giulia, Brody wondered about the whereabouts of his wee wren. It seemed odd she wasn't down here already. He hoped she wasn't ill. She'd seemed perfectly fine that morning.

The atmosphere in the room had turned convivial by the time Ugolino signaled to the servants to bring in a large crate. Fergus had ordered champagne to be served and seemed reconciled to Giulia's arrival. Marina and the contessa sat together on a sofa and conversed in Italian with every sign of amity. The rest of the party appeared to have recovered from their surprise at the newcomers' unheralded arrival.

Yet still no Elspeth.

Brody leaned on the mantelpiece above the blazing fire and leveled a disgruntled eye on the cheerful crowd. Most years, he was happy to see everyone at Christmas. This year, he could muster no interest in anyone except Hamish's sister.

Hamish sauntered over to join him. "You're in the doldrums tonight, laddie."

While Hamish was Scottish, he'd been brought up in London and educated at Eton and Cambridge. As a result, he was almost aggressively nationalist and determined to prove his credentials as a Highlander. Even if he spoke in a crisp English accent that put Brody more in mind of Mayfair than Inverness.

"I'm feeling cooped up," Brody said, although that was the least of what troubled him.

"Aye. The weather hasn't been kind. Ugolino and his countess are lucky they made it through. They must have been desperate to get to Achnasheen before Christmas."

Desperate to present Marina and Fergus with a fait accompli at a time of year that encouraged goodwill to all, Brody guessed. "Where's your sister?"

Hamish cast him a curious look. "Elspeth?"

Irritation made Brody exhale in a hiss through his teeth. "Of course bloody Elspeth."

"How the devil would I know? She and Marina have been shut up together most of the day."

That at least explained his failure to find her. Hamish stared at him in dawning comprehension. "Don't tell me you're harboring wicked intentions toward Elspeth. I'd be sorry to have to shoot one of my best friends on the field of honor."

"I wouldn't seduce a chum's sister." Brody shifted in discomfort, because given the opportunity, he feared that was just what he might do. "I have some integrity."

"See that you keep your hands to yourself." Hamish paused. "Not that Elspeth is likely to do anything silly for the sake of you asking. She might act like a wee mouse, but she's a strong-minded lassie and no fool."

Brody cast his friend a look of dislike. "She's far from a mouse. You and your family underestimate her. Ye always have."

"Always, is it?" Mocking amazement lifted Hamish's dark blond eyebrows. "Just when did you start to take note of my sister's finer qualities? I'd wager half Glen Lyon that a month ago, you didn't even know her name."

"Then you'd lose," Brody said shortly.

"Good God, you're serious about this nonsense." The astonishment widening Hamish's bright blue eyes turned genuine. "You've set your sights on quiet wee Elspeth."

Had he? Something had changed in the last few days. He found himself thinking of Elspeth in ways that he'd never thought of another woman. Her subtle beauty drew him under her spell. More than that, he liked her. Her sweetness offered welcome rest to his turbulent soul.

He met his friend's steady gaze and spoke with a conviction that surprised him. "If I did, would ye have any objection?"

Hamish frowned into his champagne glass and didn't come up with the ready answer Brody wanted. By the time he responded, Brody felt ready to explode.

"Brody, I like you," he said slowly. "You know I do. We've been friends for years. In our time, we've spent many a wild evening carousing together."

His gut knotting with resentment and hurt, Brody scowled at the man he hoped would become his brother-in-law. "If I marry your sister, I'll put all that behind me."

"An easy promise to make." Hamish still looked troubled. "A harder promise to keep."

Brody sighed. He supposed he deserved this. But it was lowering to discover that neither Diarmid nor Hamish, men he'd always considered his friends, thought him a worthy suitor for Elspeth.

"I've kicked up my heels like any young man, but you must agree there's no real vice in me. I'll make Elspeth a good husband, I swear. If I don't, I'll let ye bloody well shoot me."

This extravagant offer didn't lighten Hamish's somber demeanor. "It's very sudden."

"That doesnae make it wrong. Look at Ugolino and Giulia. Anyway I've known the lassie for years."

"Which is why I wonder what's changed."

Brody shrugged and admitted the unpalatable truth. "Perhaps it's time for me to grow up."

Hamish sighed. "I'm still not convinced this isn't some passing fancy. You've been in a devilish odd humor this last year or so."

Brody was surprised his friend had noticed. He thought he'd hidden his gnawing discontentment. "Are ye saying you dinnae give me permission to court your sister?"

"It's up to Elspeth whether she'll have you." For the first time, a hint of amusement entered Hamish's bright blue eyes. "If you can persuade her that you're the one for her, I won't stand in your way."

Relief made Brody sag, relief so powerful that he was glad that the mantelpiece was close enough to offer him its support. "That's dashed sporting of ye." His eyes narrowed on his friend's face. "Except you dinnae think she will take me, do ye?"

Hamish shrugged, unperturbed by Brody's accusation. "If she does, it's because she sees more in you than I ever have. She's a level-headed lassie, my sister. Bonny words and a bonny face alone won't convince her to trust herself to a laddie."

"I know," Brody said, then he couldn't help voicing his chagrin. "I didnae ken ye harbored such a low opinion of me."

Hamish's expression was uncharacteristically austere. "You're a braw companion for a night in the stews. But now you're talking about marrying my sister."

"I am," he said, and despite Hamish's unexpected objections, something inside him firmed and settled. At last he had his hand on the tiller, and he set sail in the right direction.

Brody looked around at that moment and felt no surprise when he saw Elspeth standing in the doorway. She was his destination, his harbor, his sanctuary. The woman who would make sense of his chaotic, purposeless life.

Then he looked at her properly, and his heart took a sickening dive into his boots. Bloody Marina. He could strangle the sloe-eyed besom. With her help and within the space of a day, his wee wren had transformed into someone new, and all Brody's happy certainties crashed around him in ruins.

# CHAPTER SEVEN

In front of the mirror upstairs, Elspeth had been delighted with the transformation Marina and Sandra had worked on her. She'd stared at the pretty girl reflected back and decided there would be no more slinking around in the shadows for her.

But as dinner approached, her courage ebbed, and she'd needed to summon every last scrap of willpower to force herself to go downstairs. What if everyone hated the changes in her appearance?

What if everyone liked them?

Somehow that seemed worse, an indictment of the person she'd been all her life.

She made it downstairs at the last minute and steeled herself to enter the drawing room, only to discover nobody paid her any attention at all. Marina's father, a man she'd met once before, had arrived with a lady she didn't know, and the air was alive with celebration.

"Elspeth, you missed the news," Prudence said, coming up and passing her a glass of champagne. "Ugolino has brought his new wife to us for

Christmas, without giving anyone the least warning."

The Italian lady across the room was small and round, and dressed in expensive, stylish clothes. At her side, Ugolino was unmistakably enamored.

"How nice for him," she said, both relieved and disappointed that she'd managed to sneak into the room unnoticed. "How did Marina take the news?"

"She was surprised, like all of us. But now she and Giulia seem to be getting on famously." Prudence lowered her voice. "I did worry that Fergus might knock Ugolino down, when he wandered in as cool as a cucumber and announced the marriage. It was pretty clear that Marina was trying to hide her shock at having a new stepmother."

Near the windows, Marina stood with her husband, her father, and her father's bride. If she was still upset, she did a good job of hiding it.

Prudence cast Elspeth a quick glance, then another more comprehensive one. "You look nice. Have you changed your hair?"

Elspeth choked back a disbelieving laugh. A whole day of primping and preening, and that was the best Prudence could do? "I wanted to try something a little different."

"It suits you. You should wear it like that all the time."

Prudence drifted off to find Charles. The crowd shifted. Elspeth found herself looking straight at Brody Girvan, who regarded her with an unreadable expression on his hawkish face. She raised an unsteady hand to the tumble of loose curls Sandra had spent an hour arranging. Upstairs she'd loved the effect, thinking it made her look poised and sophisticated. Perhaps she was wrong about that. Perhaps she just looked absurd.

Brody strode across the room to her. "You look splendid, Elspeth," he said, raising his glass in her direction.

She frowned. His tone contained an edge that she didn't quite understand. "Marina has been giving me some advice."

"God bless Marina," he said and emptied his glass.

"Don't...don't you like it?" Then cursed herself for sounding so lily-livered. What did it matter if Brody approved or not? She hadn't gone to this trouble for his sake, but for her own.

"Devil take me, of course I damn well do." The detailed survey he made of her burned, and she hid a shiver of feminine awareness. Those assessing eyes didn't miss a single inch of the newly transformed Elspeth Douglas. "But you can't blame a man for regretting that you're no longer his secret treasure."

Her eyes rounded, as she struggled to make sense of that astonishing remark. Brody developed a habit of leaving her speechless. Marina had said she looked pretty, and something in Brody's unwavering attention told her he agreed. The confidence that had faltered as she faced an audience began to revive.

"What do you—"

The rest of the question was lost as Ugolino clapped his hands to gain the crowd's attention. "*Grazie tante. Grazie a tutti. Troppo gentile. Grazie mille*. Thank you for the warm welcome you have given to my beautiful bride Giulia and to me on this cold Scottish night."

Elspeth hid a smile. Given what Prudence had said, Ugolino was putting a gloss on his reception when he arrived. Fergus must have been livid at the tactless way his father-in-law introduced the newest member of the family.

Ugolino continued. "Many years ago, Marina's mamma introduced me to a charming English Christmas custom that I'd like to bring north of the border." He nodded at the liveried Italian footmen—presumably the contessa's servants—standing beside a large crate in the corner. Elspeth hadn't noticed it before. "With much difficulty and copious correspondence, I arranged for this to be waiting in Glasgow when we arrived."

She craned her head to see as the servants opened the crate to reveal white sheeting. When Ugolino stepped forward and flung aside the material, he uncovered nests of green leaves and white berries.

"Mistletoe..." Elspeth said at the same time as Marina spoke.

"Papa, what a wonderful gift." Marina turned to Fergus. "It was a seasonal tradition in Mamma's family home in England when she grew up. You hang it about the house, and if anyone is standing under it, they get a kiss. It makes for a lot of fun and silliness over Christmas."

Fergus looked puzzled and not unduly impressed. "It sounds like a mad Sassenach notion to me."

She darted forward to pluck a sprig and hold it above her head. She fluttered her eyelashes in an exaggerated fashion. "Pray, won't you kiss me, kind sir?"

Fergus laughed and grabbed her by the waist. "Aye, I'll kiss ye, lassie, but I dinnae need permission first from someone waving an English weed in the air."

He pressed his lips to hers, then smiled at his father-in-law with no trace of any earlier hostility. "My wife is in favor of your offering."

Ugolino smiled back and snatched up a sprig of his own. "Tomorrow we'll hang the mistletoe around the house, and the kissing can begin. But first, let me kiss my bride."

Giulia looked charmingly ruffled when he released her, and Elspeth was surprised to catch an approving smile on Brody's face. She would have thought all this nonsense was too rustic and unsophisticated to divert a rake of his reputation. "Did you already know about this tradition?"

He shook his dark head. "No. It's no' a plant that grows hereabouts. If it gives me an excuse to kiss ye, I'm all in favor."

"I'd better be careful where I stand, then," she retorted, struggling with further amazement at the idea that he wanted to kiss her, mistletoe or not.

"Aye, make sure it's right under the mistletoe."

She ignored that, although the prospect of Brody's kisses made her breathless with excitement. Of course they did. She'd never been kissed, and after his adventures with all those loose women, he should be good at it. Her kissing career would start with a master of the art. When she fell in love for real, she'd have grounds for comparison. "We always hang it in our London house if we're down there for Christmas."

He arched a sleek eyebrow at her, and the glint of mischief in his eyes made her heart stutter. "Are ye saying you're an old hand at this kissing game?"

Once, yesterday even, she might have found herself blushing and stammering, but the admiration in his eyes gave her the nerve to tease him back. "That's for me to know and you to find out."

"You've kissed hundreds of men, I'm sure."

"Perhaps not hundreds." She'd been a little girl when the family hosted Christmas parties in

London. Her father had still been alive, and any kissing had been a childish game, like bobbing for apples or snapdragon.

"I look forward to seeing what ye can teach me."

"Not much, I'm sure." She narrowed her eyes on him. "I've heard the gossip."

To her surprise, he didn't laugh. "A man can turn over a new leaf." He paused. "With the right incentive."

"What are you saying?" she said, her fingers tightening on her champagne glass and her heart rising to stick in her throat like a lump of soggy tapioca.

He glanced around, then lowered his voice, although from what she could see, nobody paid them a scrap of attention. "I'll tell ye once I get you alone under the mistletoe. At last something useful comes out of England."

"Brody..." she said, not sure whether she meant to protest or encourage him. For a girl who had foresworn all interest in him, this was a dangerous game to play.

She stared up into green eyes that seemed to send her a private message. It took her a few moments to realize that her mother had come up to join them. "Elspeth, you look lovely tonight."

The intensity drained from Brody's expression, and he was once again the urbane gentleman who charmed all the ladies, with no thoughts of settling for one in particular. "Lady Glen Lyon, Elspeth always looks lovely."

Her mother smiled at him. "You're such a charming fellow, Brody." She checked back on her daughter. "You've changed your hair."

"Marina lent me her maid for the evening."

Her mother patted her own elegant blond knot. "Perhaps she'll give me some pointers. She's made quite the difference to you, my dear." She frowned. "And is that a new dress? I don't recall seeing it before."

Elspeth glanced down at the dark blue silk she'd worn a hundred times and hid a smile. Marina and Sandra had done her proud. Instead of a plain gown that buttoned like a noose against her throat, Sandra's magic scissors had created a flattering square décolletage that revealed more flesh than she was used to showing.

Despite Elspeth's protests at the extravagant gift, Marina had produced some exquisite Brussels lace to soften the dress's stark lines. The soft, buttery color lent a creamy tinge to her skin. She'd already noticed how Brody's eyes dwelled on her exposed bosom, but was cynical enough to know that libertines were in the habit of inspecting a lady's breasts. He wouldn't think her bosom anything special.

"It's something old I had altered," she said, touching the gold locket that dangled at her throat. It had been her grandmother's, and she didn't wear it often. Her previous style of gown didn't call for much jewelry.

"I should lend you my sapphires. They'd look perfect with that color. I'm pleased to see you paying more attention to your appearance. You've never been interested before."

"Doesn't Elspeth look lovely tonight?" Marina came up and smiled at her protégée with open approval.

"Breathtaking," Brody said with what seemed like genuine fervor, and Elspeth had to remind herself that compliments were part of a rake's arsenal. He didn't mean anything beyond politeness, even if it sounded like he did.

"She does." To Elspeth's astonishment, her mother leaned in and kissed her cheek. "I have to congratulate you, Marina. However I tried, I never managed to prize my daughter away from those dreadful dowdy frocks. She's always been my cuckoo in the nest. In Town, I could never keep Grace, Prudence and Charity out of the shops, and I could barely get Elspeth into one."

"We can go shopping next time we're in Edinburgh," Elspeth said in a tentative tone and was surprised at her mother's immediate enthusiasm. Perhaps she'd become a little too comfortable with her place as the family afterthought, and perhaps her mother's benign neglect wasn't altogether the result of selfishness.

"I'd like that very much."

Elspeth listened with half an ear as Mamma and Marina discussed Italian fashions, while she wondered if this new look might improve her relations with her mother. It wasn't what she'd expected, but it was a change she'd welcome.

# CHAPTER EIGHT

By the time Brody sat down to dinner, he was almost in charity with his hostess. The fact that Marina had placed him next to Elspeth went a long way toward softening his resentment. As did Elspeth's palpable amazement at the flood of compliments she'd received on her changed appearance. Amazement and blossoming pleasure. Ugolino and Giulia remained the center of attention, but nobody missed how stylish young Miss Douglas looked in midnight blue silk and cream lace.

Brody had no right to feel disgruntled. On Elspeth's behalf, he'd come to resent the way her family overlooked her. But some unworthy element in him had gloated to know that only he was perceptive enough to notice her beauty and charm.

"What is it?" she asked under her breath, as fish replaced the soup course and the party's happy chatter buzzed about them.

"Pardon?" he asked.

"You keep staring at me."

"You're a lassie worth staring at."

Those full, pink lips tightened in displeasure. "You never thought that before."

He cast her an unimpressed glance and cut into his fillet of sole in lemon sauce. "You know that's nae true. I stared at ye well before you decided to turn into a diamond of the first water."

Self-consciously, she touched the elaborate arrangement of curls framing her face. "Don't you approve?"

With a grunt of amusement, he raised his glass of hock in a mocking toast that at heart wasn't mocking at all. "Dinnae be a daft wee widgeon, Elspeth. Of course I approve. You're beautiful."

Faint rose tinged her cheeks, and her eyelashes fluttered down. "Thank you."

"I like what you've done with your hair. It makes me want to take ye to bed."

She gave a soft gasp, and her gaze whipped back to his face. "You're being wicked again. You just can't help yourself."

He shrugged. "When I see ye, I certainly can't. I imagine that's the reaction Marina's maid aimed to create." He paused. "Although to be fair, I wanted to take ye to bed when your hair was pulled back so tightly, it made me wince. And I definitely commend whatever sorcery you've accomplished with yon blue dress. I always thought you had a magnificent bosom. Now the rest of the world can see enough of ye to agree with me."

The rose deepened, and the magnificent bosom swelled most impressively. He braced for a scolding. He deserved one. After all, he was behaving like a cad, considering she was an innocent and his friend's sister, and he was sitting at the family dinner table. But he loved the way her eyes flashed when he teased her. That hadn't changed, despite her dressing to dazzle.

But instead of delivering a set down, Elspeth regarded him curiously. "Do you never have a normal, sensible discussion with a woman? Something about—I don't know—what she did today, or her family, or the books she's read? Is it always this flirtatious nonsense?"

Under her probing gaze, he shifted in discomfort. Especially because, while it was sadly true that his usual banter with females was nonsense, when he told Elspeth he wanted her, it wasn't nonsense at all. "You dinnae like it?"

Brody waited for her to say no. To his surprise, her eyes flickered away again and she concentrated on her meal. "Of course I like it. I'm as susceptible as any other woman to a handsome man's flattery—as you very well know, or you wouldn't do it. But all this teasing and taunting make it impossible to know you in any genuine way. Perhaps that's why you do it."

"What a bleak assessment." His lips turned down, as he endured another, sharper pang of discomfort. Her perception wasn't altogether welcome. "But be fair, lassie. I ken what ye did all day. I ken everything I need to about your family. If we discuss books, you'll discover how woefully ignorant I am, and decide I'm no' worth your trouble. I cannae allow that. What else is there? I could tell ye some scandalous stories about my last visit to Edinburgh, but they're nae suitable for polite company."

"Would you really?" To his surprise, he caught a spark of interest in her expression as she looked up from her fish. "I'd love to know more about the demimonde."

His lips twisted in a wry smile. "Ye probably wouldn't."

"But you might tell me later?"

"I might. But where does that leave us now? I could talk about your bosom."

Her turn for a wry smile. "You've certainly spent long enough looking at it."

"It merits a lifetime of study," he said ardently, every word sincere.

After shooting him a dismissive glance, her expression turned serious. "You could tell me about Invermackie. I've never been there, and I've always been curious about it."

He shook his head in bafflement. "You're a strange girl."

She smiled. "A new hairstyle hasn't changed me that much."

He smiled back. "So I see."

She took a sip of white wine. "Is Invermackie like Glen Lyon?"

"Well, it's a Highland estate, with hills and lochs and a view over the sea, but that's about as far as the similarity goes. It's wild and isolated, a glen with a secret harbor looking straight across at the hills of Harris. The river starts with waterfalls high up the brae behind the house, and rushes down from Loch Mackie to meet the sea."

The brown eyes turned velvety in a way they never did when he tried to seduce her with compliments, damn it. "It sounds beautiful."

"Aye, it is. When the north wind isn't howling about your ears and turning them blue." Actually even in dreich weather, he thought his home was beautiful, but he didn't expect the opinion to gain general acceptance.

Elspeth made a dismissive sound. "That's true about the whole of Scotland. We all know the nice days make up for the horrible ones. Tell me more."

Brody set down his cutlery and stared into space, his head full of the spectacular place where he was born.

"I grew up at Invermackie House. It's built beside a beach of golden sand, just perfect for a run with a dog or a gallop on a swift horse. If you're lucky, you'll see otters and eagles and seals and dolphins. In hidden hollows, ancient trees still grow. There's a local superstition that if the forest disappears from the estate, the lairds will, too. That gives us a vested interest in keeping it alive. The people of Invermackie in the village and on the crofts are hardy, and there's sea salt in their veins and in their conversation. The soil is thin, and the land is only good for raising sheep and cattle, but the sea has been generous to us. There's a fine living in the fishing. If ye ever tried an Invermackie smoked herring, you'd scorn my cousin's fine trout as second rate." Brody came back to the moment to see her lips twitch.

"Don't tell Fergus," she said.

"I willnae." Heat flooded his cheeks. "I'm sorry. I seem to be waxing lyrical, and while I rant like a loon, your dinner is getting cold."

"Thank you for telling me all that." The eyes she turned on him glowed with interest. "It sounds wonderful."

"You wouldn't think that, when the blizzards shriek around the house in January," Brody muttered, before he recalled his plans to make Elspeth the lady of Invermackie. Perhaps it might be politic to avoid too much discussion of the weather.

"A good excuse to stay inside by the hearth."

He had a sudden vivid image of Elspeth in the parlor at Invermackie House, with a roaring fire in the grate. The wind might shriek around the rafters like a banshee, but he wouldn't give a farthing about anything except the bonny woman on his knee. His gut clenched on a longing that was almost painful. He wanted that dream to come true more than he'd ever wanted anything in his hedonistic life.

"Aye, it is at that. May I mention beds again?"

"No, you may not." Her disapproval was charming. "Tell me more about the house."

"It's nae a castle like Achnasheen, but bonny for all that. Old gray stone, mullioned windows that open onto the sea, big, airy rooms paneled in dark wood." He glanced around his cousin's dining room, decorated in fashionable gold and green stripes, and smiled. "A few modern notions wouldnae go astray, if I'm honest. The place desperately needs a woman's touch. My mother wasnae much given to fashionable taste, before she passed away thirteen years ago. My father believed in tradition and liked things to stay as they'd always been."

"How long have you been the laird?"

"Since I was twenty-three. Two years ago now."

"Time enough to change the décor."

"I'm rarely there."

She frowned. "That's sad, when you love it so much."

He did. Every rugged, barren, windswept, gorgeous inch of it. "It's easier to play the rake in Edinburgh than the laird at Invermackie," he said, before he remembered that mentioning his roguish reputation wasn't the best way to promote his suitability as a husband. "The estate is a long way away from everything."

A long way away? That was an understatement. Invermackie was two days' ride north of Achnasheen. And Achnasheen was the arse end of nowhere.

"If it's what you want, it's right where it needs to be," she said softly, but with breathtaking certainty. Her wisdom struck him silent, as he wondered if she'd ever see the home he cherished.

On her other side, Donald made a remark about the bad weather. With her habitual good manners, Elspeth turned to reply to her brother-in-law. Without much remorse, Brody admitted that he'd been monopolizing her. Giulia sat next to him, but she and Ugolino were busy making sheep's eyes at one another.

Brody stared down at his fish and thought about what Elspeth had said. She was right. Why the devil was he ready to exile himself from his home and waste his youth in tawdry pursuits? Not that the pursuits had felt tawdry at the time. He'd thoroughly enjoyed his libertine days, but he was well overdue to move on to more mature activities.

After his father's death, Invermackie had seemed lonely and empty, and Brody had left it to escape his grief. He'd also felt like an imposter whenever anyone addressed him as the laird. As far as Brody was concerned, the laird was his father, even if he lay buried in the churchyard.

But for the last two years, the house had waited in its hidden glen for him to return and fill it with family and laughter and joy. At last, now he'd settled his interest on Elspeth, he saw a chance for that to happen.

As he started to eat, he prayed his wee wren would marry him, and live on his estate, and turn the sad, empty shell of Invermackie House into a home once more.

The party went late, as the guests lingered downstairs to celebrate Ugolino and Giulia's nuptials. By the time Elspeth had danced her last reel and sung her last Christmas carol, she was weary. Not to mention a little unsteady on her feet. She wasn't used to strong spirits, and Fergus had encouraged her to toast the happy couple with a dram or two of whisky.

She remained keyed up. It had been a long day, brimming with excitement and nerves. And compliments on her appearance, although the admiration in Brody's eyes had done the most to convince her that the change was to her advantage.

How she'd enjoyed their talk at dinner. What an interesting man he was, once he sloughed off the rakish shell. She mightn't pine after him anymore, but she appreciated a chance to know him better. The longing in his voice as he spoke of Invermackie had made her ache to race over those golden sands with him at her side.

He said he headed home after Hogmanay. She hoped when he did, he found the peace he sought. Because somewhere in the last few days, she'd come to see that despite his carefully cultivated air of insouciance, he was unhappy. She wished she could do something to ease his care—purely as a friend. Despite his teasing remarks about kissing, she'd relinquished all ambitions to become his lover.

Perhaps they inched toward a genuine friendship now because she'd given up her romantic dreams. Before this, she'd been too shy and adoring to engage him in anything approaching a real conversation.

As the guests drifted through the holly-bedecked hall in search of their beds, Elspeth looked for Brody. She'd love to hear more about Invermackie and what it had been like to grow up there. But he must have already gone upstairs. Or more likely he'd sneaked away to smoke a cigar and escape the endless seasonal cheer. He wasn't a man who liked an early night, she'd noticed.

Still, it was disappointing not to wish him good night and bask in his presence. Some female element inside her couldn't help responding to the seductive charm in those green eyes, so striking with his ruffled dark hair.

Feeling a little out of sorts, which was odd when she'd spent the rest of the evening on top of the world, she trudged toward the stairs. Then she started as a strong hand curled around her arm.

"Come away with me, lassie," a husky voice murmured in her ear. "The evening's no' over for ye yet, wee Elspeth. Not by a long shot."

# CHAPTER NINE

"Brody," Elspeth squeaked, doing nothing to stop him from hauling her into the morning room to the left of the magnificent carved oak staircase. "What on earth are you doing?"

"Whisht, lassie," he whispered. "We've only got a minute. If you're late upstairs, people will want to ken why."

When she shivered, she wasn't sure whether it was from cold or excitement. Through the fine silk of her dress, his grip on her waist was possessive and warm. The morning room, on the other hand, wasn't. The fire was only lit in here during the day.

"I want to know why, too," she said, although she kept her voice to a murmur.

He held up a sprig of something green and waved it in front of her nose. "I want to test out Ugolino's magic plant."

This time the shiver was definitely a thrill. A handsome laird bustled her away to steal a kiss. What a perfect end to an evening where nobody had even thought to call her a mouse. "You want to kiss me?"

"I do indeed." She caught the flash of a reckless smile, before he pushed the door shut and trapped her in darkness vibrant with anticipation. In the closed room, the scent of pine from the Christmas greenery around the walls was heady enough to make her dizzy.

Or perhaps the pine branches had nothing at all to do with her giddiness.

"I've never been kissed," she said softly.

His groan came from somewhere above her. He'd moved closer. Her eyes slowly adjusted, and she made out the shape of his tall, lean body against the black. "Dinnae say things like that. What about all those kisses under the mistletoe ye told me about?"

"I was about six. I don't think they count." She paused. "I suppose you think it's shocking that I've never kissed a man the way a woman does."

"No, not shocking, arousing." When he shaped his hands around her face, the air jammed in her throat. "And cruel when I only have ye to myself for a minute or two."

The hands cradling her face were unsteady, and he was close enough for her to hear the erratic rhythm of his breath. In her wildest dreams, she'd never imagined Brody Girvan saying such things or shaking with need for her.

The Brody of her girlish fantasies had been a poor-spirited creature, who spouted bad poetry and begged for the privilege of holding her hand. The real version was much more dynamic and enthralling. It was a good thing she didn't love him anymore, or she'd be quite beside herself and likely to do something stupid.

"You'd better make the most of the opportunity," she was startled to hear herself say. The old Elspeth would never have found the nerve to encourage a young man's attentions. It seemed changing her hair and clothes had changed a few other things as well.

And about time, too.

"Ye don't have to ask twice, my bonny." With a husky laugh, he tilted her face up and brushed his lips across hers.

Her first kiss. And from a beautiful man like Brody. How utterly...marvelous. A tingling thrill rippled through her, tightening her skin and making her toes curl in their blue satin slippers. She twined her arms around his neck and tangled her fingers in the silky hair at the base of his skull.

Another touch of his lips drew a yearning whimper from her, and she stretched up to get closer. This time, he lingered over the kiss, flicking his tongue along the seam of her lips.

Elspeth was trembling, and her knees felt likely to collapse. Had she said she was cold? She doubted she'd ever be cold again. Delicious heat licked along her veins and made her feel strange and wonderful. And powerful.

Brody released her face and lashed his arms around her, dragging her into his body. The kiss became more intent, and instinctively she parted her lips, seeking more of his taste. He gave a deep growl of satisfaction, and his tongue slipped through to dance against hers.

How bizarre. Elspeth made a muffled protest and stiffened, while the waves of tremulous pleasure washing through her turned to throbbing need.

He raised his head, and when he spoke, his breath was warm on her face. She caught the smoky honey tinge of Fergus's whisky, the same flavor she'd tasted on Brody's lips. "This is torture. I want to keep ye here forever."

She'd started to yearn up toward him again, before she realized what he'd said.

"I can't stay." She didn't try to hide her regret.

"I know." He sounded no happier than she did. "But there's always tomorrow."

Distantly she heard the clock in the hall strike two, followed a few seconds later by the delicate tinkle of the ormolu clock on the mantelpiece in this room. "Today."

"Even better." The thicker brogue told her he was smiling. "But I still dinnae want to let ye go."

Despite her innocence, despite his expressed good intentions, she knew that with one word's encouragement, he'd have her flat on her back on the chaise longue. Difficult as it was to remember while she quivered in his arms, she'd kissed Brody as an experiment, not as part of a life-changing commitment.

"You must." Daringly she rose on her toes and kissed him briefly on the lips. Then she slid her arms free and turned to crack open the door.

"Is it safe for us to go?" he murmured, trailing swift kisses along her nape. Lightning bolts of sensation sizzled through her, and her breath caught on a stifled moan. Who knew her neck was such a sensitive area?

"Yes..." She paused, then pushed the door forward until only a sliver of light shone through. "No."

"Are ye truly at peace with your father's choice, *mo chridhe*?" Fergus's deep voice was clearly audible from the hall outside.

"*Si, certo,*" Marina said. She and her husband were standing at the base of the staircase, by the sound of it. "It was a surprise, of course, but Giulia seems a good woman, and there's no doubt that they love one another."

"Aye, he's smitten, all right. But ye and Ugolino were alone together as a family for a long time. This woman is stepping into your mother's place."

"*Caro*, you're sweet to worry about me."

"Of course I worry about you, ye mutton-headed lassie. I love you."

"And I love you, Mackinnon."

There was a pause, when Elspeth guessed that the couple kissed. It was a private moment. She shifted uncomfortably and felt Brody's arm slide around her waist. He bent to nibble another line of kisses across the back of her neck, and she bit back a gasp as a wealth of nerve-endings stirred into charged life. Her nipples hardened against the soft lawn of her shift, and the secret places in her body softened and turned liquid.

"Stop it," she said on a breath.

As she should have expected, that provoked another kiss, this time under her hairline. Her knees wobbled, and she sagged, grateful that his powerful arm held her upright. It would be too humiliating to crumple into a heap of feminine enjoyment at his feet.

"He could have broken the news better," Fergus said with a hint of grimness.

"Knowing Papa, he hoped to avoid a scene by presenting us with a fait accompli. Anyway, he did give me some warning. Before we married, he told me that he was going back to Florence to find a nice, comfortable widow. I'd been too selfish to see that he was lonely, traveling around with just me for company."

"Och, you have such a generous heart, Marina. Ye put me to shame."

"*Cielo*, come upstairs with me now, and if you're good, I'll show you just how generous I am, my fine Highland laird."

He laughed softly. "I'm always good, *mo leannan*. Haven't ye worked that out yet?"

"Oh, so arrogant!" Their voices faded as they climbed the steps. "It's lucky for you that you're charming along with it."

Once she was sure Marina and Fergus had left, Elspeth cautiously opened the door. "I have to go, before the servants start snuffing the candles."

"I know," Brody said, the heat of his body burning along her back. He kissed her neck again with predictable results. Dear heaven, how on earth would she sleep after all this excitement?

"Will you stop doing that?" she hissed, shifting against him and making him groan.

"Ye like it."

"Of course I like it," she said impatiently. "That's the problem."

He laughed.

"Shh!"

He lowered his voice again. "I'll see ye tomorrow?"

"Of course."

He still didn't let go, although his hold loosened. She could get away if she wanted, but right now, she was having too good a time. The prospect of her departure made him miserable. How glorious. After he'd disregarded her for so long, she couldn't help basking in his sudden interest.

"Alone like this?"

"We'll see." In all the years that she'd longed for Brody Girvan across an unbridgeable distance, she'd never imagined she'd feel brave enough to tease him. Tonight, the distance shrank to nothing at all.

She knew what they did was a game. Neither of them took it seriously. But she'd loved his kisses, and she hoped to heaven he'd kiss her again before Christmas was over.

The wish came true faster than she'd expected. Brody twisted her around and kissed her lips. "You should go."

"I should." Really she'd have to do something about reinforcing her legs, if he was going to make a habit of kissing her. Her knees were back to imitating wet string. "Good night, Brody."

"Good night, *mo chridhe.*"

She stiffened in his grasp. He called her his heart, and she knew he didn't mean it the way Fergus did when he used the endearment to Marina. Even an innocent like Elspeth understood that insincere avowals were part of a flirtation, but this one cut a little too close to the bone.

Her voice was shaky when she spoke. "Carry your mistletoe when next we meet."

"It's in my pocket, and that's where it will stay." His lilting Highland accent warmed and deepened.

"Good. You never know, it may come in handy." She paused. "Then again, it may not."

"Elspeth, ye wee besom..."

She disentangled herself, and this time slipped out of the morning room without his interference. Brody didn't follow, which turned out to be fortunate. The maids, Kirsty and Rowena, emerged from the hall carrying trays of dirty glasses.

Elspeth wished the girls good night and prayed that the frail candlelight was kind enough to hide any evidence that she'd just enjoyed a thorough kissing from a roguish laird.

Or perhaps not quite thorough enough. She shivered again—it had been quite a shivery evening all round—to recall that strange, but wildly thrilling moment when his tongue had dipped into her mouth. She'd never imagined anyone doing such a thing, but tasting him so deeply, however fleeting the incursion, had sparked her carnal interest. What she'd felt in Brody's arms was a million miles away from her milksop fantasies.

At least tonight had banished those juvenile absurdities forever. Her difficulty now was to avoid becoming addicted to his touch—and to make sure that he didn't mistake her willingness to swap a few playful kisses for a desire to take things further. If he compromised her here at a family party, a proposal would be the inevitable result.

Pursuing a flirtation and preserving her virtue required a risky balance, for his sake and hers. Elspeth had no intention of accepting a reluctant bridegroom.

Her sensual curiosity must remain unsatisfied. A conclusion both unwelcome and inescapable.

But more kisses? More kisses, if she was careful, should be safe enough.

As she stepped onto the landing at the top of the staircase and headed for her room on feet lighter than air, her lips curved in a greedy smile.

# CHAPTER TEN

The next day, the weather improved enough to permit the promised riding excursion. Brody was happy to get out of the castle. However large the accommodations, days cooped up inside were difficult for a man of active habits. He welcomed the opportunity to gallop across the snowy hillsides, and cast his eyes over the wide vistas of his cousin's estate, and breathe air straight off the top of the mountains.

Not to mention that a ride in the open might provide a chance to coax Elspeth away for more kisses.

It was years since he'd pursued a lady with no purpose beyond kissing. To his shame, he had to go back to when he was fourteen and madly in love with the miller's pretty daughter at Invermackie.

Pretty Polly Macrae was still as plump as a pigeon. She lived happily on the estate, with her husband John Robertson, the blacksmith, and four red-headed children. While Brody's interest in Polly had long since faded, he'd retained his early weakness for a soft armful of sweet woman. A soft armful like Elspeth Douglas. Why the devil had he taken this long to notice that Hamish's sister was perfect for him?

The prospect of possessing her had kept him awake and itching with frustration most of the night. But he was prepared to master his impatience and wait until she was lawfully his. Then heaven help her, he'd set out to slake an appetite that only grew more powerful after last night's tormenting, delightful kisses.

When he lured her into the morning room, he'd known that they only had minutes together. He needed to keep a tight rein on his passions. That plan had lasted about ten seconds, until the first innocent touch of her lips. He'd gone up in a roar of flame, while the temptation to devour her mouth and explore that luscious body had nearly overmastered him. Surely Satan himself had sculpted those sinuous curves.

He'd managed to act like a gentleman—or as much of a gentleman as a laddie could, when kissing a well-bred female behind a closed door. But maintaining his restraint had tried him to the limit. Once Elspeth promised to marry him, she'd better get ready for a quick ceremony. Or else he very much feared she'd be no virgin on her wedding night.

"Are ye all right, cuz?" Fergus asked curiously, trotting up on the big gray mare he always rode.

"I didn't sleep too well," Brody admitted.

His steamy fantasies of Elspeth kept him lagging behind the rest of the group. Ahead, riders strung out across the snowy hillside. Everyone had come outside this afternoon, except Ugolino and Giulia, who rested after their long journey. The children were chasing one another on their ponies. Prudence and Charity rode together, with Lady Glen Lyon a little further back beside Donald and Charles. Marina cantered ahead of the pack. Brody was surprised Fergus wasn't riding at her side as he usually did.

Elspeth had set out with the others. Now he couldn't see her.

Nor could he see Diarmid. Suspicion jabbed him with a sharp fork. Was she practicing her new kissing skills with her handsome cousin? Brody decided then and there, he'd brook no delay in getting his ring on the lassie's finger. Tomorrow was Christmas Eve. What better day to make a proposal?

He wasn't by nature a romantic, but he knew Elspeth was. All those books she devoured were crammed with deeds of derring-do and larger-than-life heroes. He needed to ask for her hand with suitable panache.

Once she consented, just let that snake Diarmid try and look at her sideways. He'd beat the bastard to a pulp.

"Did ye hear me?" Fergus asked.

With a shock, Brody realized his thoughts had drifted away. Not since the days of Polly had any female distracted him like this. "What did ye say?"

"Actually I was saying you're nae yourself this Christmas. What just happened proves it. Is there something wrong?"

Brody had assumed he'd concealed his recent restlessness from his friends. It turned out he'd assumed wrongly. "I'm thinking of making a few changes."

"A new mistress?"

He couldn't blame Fergus for jumping to that conclusion. With a sigh, he decided to confess his plans. After all, he'd told Hamish. Fergus also deserved to know. "A new wife."

"Och, that's braw news." Fergus looked delighted. "Are congratulations due, old man? Who's the lucky lassie? I hadn't heard of ye courting anyone. I assume she's a lady you met in Edinburgh."

Marina had already discerned his interest in Elspeth. He was surprised she hadn't confided that news to Fergus. "Not in Edinburgh. An old family connection."

Fergus frowned. "I cannae imagine who."

Brody frowned, too. "Elspeth Douglas, of course."

"Elspeth?" Fergus sounded surprised. And not particularly pleased. With a sinking feeling, Brody recognized a reaction akin to Hamish's.

"She's a fine lassie."

"Aye, she is."

"And she'll make a bonny wife."

"She will."

The silence that hurtled down was as bruising as a rockslide. Eventually Brody could bear it no longer. "You're going to tell me I'm too selfish and shallow to make her happy."

Fergus's chiseled features could turn dauntingly stern. He'd never looked more the Laird of Achnasheen pronouncing judgment than he did when, after a sticky pause, he replied. "I know ye better than anyone else, I believe."

"Aye," Brody said cautiously, aware that such a remark wasn't likely to lead into an expression of wholehearted support. "That's true."

"Do ye love Elspeth?"

Brody frowned again. Love? He hadn't even thought about it. "I told ye—she's just right for me."

"But do ye love her?"

"I want to make her my wife. I want to live with her until I'm old. I want her to be the mother of my bairns. If that's love, then I love her."

"Och, it's a start, I suppose." Fergus's shrewd gray eyes leveled on him. "But if you want my advice, you willnae marry that lassie unless ye love her with all your heart. It's what she deserves. If ye dinnae love her like that, you'll never make her happy."

Brody shifted uncomfortably in the saddle. He'd never had a conversation like this with his cousin. With anybody. His mother had died so long ago, and his father, while a splendid fellow and a good laird, had avoided any awkward discussion of emotions. "I mean to do right by her. I'll be faithful, despite what Hamish thinks."

Fergus's eyes sharpened. "You've spoken to Hamish?"

"Aye. He's no' in favor of the match either."

"And what does wee Elspeth say?"

His hands tightened on Perseus's reins. He hoped to hell she wasn't saying "Kiss me, Diarmid" right now. "I havenae asked her yet. She's given me cause to hope."

A girl like Elspeth wouldn't kiss a laddie unless she had honorable intentions. She wasn't a hardened flirt like Brody.

Fergus still looked like he passed sentence on a sheep-stealing crofter. "You're my cousin and my friend, Brody, but if ye break that girl's heart, I'll never forgive you."

"I'm giving up my rakish ways." Brody scowled at the big, auburn-haired man riding at his side. "I have some honor."

Fergus looked unconvinced. "There are more ways to hurt a woman than taking a mistress."

He supposed there must be, although he hadn't given the matter much thought. Which didn't mean he appreciated seeing the pity in Fergus's eyes, as if his cousin was sure Brody had no idea what he was getting into.

"I look forward to marrying Elspeth and proving to you and Hamish that I can be an exemplary husband," he responded huffily.

"See that ye do," his cousin said and urged his horse into a canter.

Brody stared unseeing after Fergus. Damn it, since marrying Marina, his cousin had love on the brain. And a few other body parts, too, he'd wager. Marina and Fergus had trouble keeping their hands off each other, even after more than a year together.

If desire equaled love, he definitely loved Elspeth. But he had a grim inkling that his cousin was talking about something more profound than mere physical pleasure. God knew what. Until now, Brody had been content to dabble at the safe edges of intense emotion. Hamish had accused him of being shallow. If there wasn't an element of truth in that, it wouldn't have hurt quite so much.

Did Brody love Elspeth? Devil if he knew.

He certainly cared enough to find her absence with Diarmid increasingly infuriating.

In which case, he should have been relieved to see her trot back into view. However she and Diarmid rode a little too close, and the amity between them was too apparent for Brody to find much comfort in her reappearance. He dug his heels into his horse's sides and galloped across to where the cousins were laughing together.

"See anything interesting?" He wanted to sound nonchalant, but the question emerged with a snide tinge that made Elspeth direct a curious gaze his way. She looked lovely. Pink-cheeked with the cold, and the rich colors of the paisley shawl draped around her head set off her brilliant dark eyes and creamy skin.

Diarmid fixed a sardonic eye upon him, as if he guessed the lurid suspicions running through

Brody's mind. "Aye, we enjoyed a delightful interlude," he said in a silken voice. "I rarely get Elspeth to myself."

To think, Brody had once considered this slimy toad his friend. His hands jerked on the reins, making Perseus sidle across the firm snow in equine protest. Elspeth's expression remained puzzled. To his relief, she didn't look like a woman who'd just been kissed.

"Diarmid was showing me the view across to Skye. You can see the Cuillins from where we were."

Bugger the Cuillins. "Indeed." Brody wished he didn't sound like a sulky schoolboy.

The three of them settled into an ambling walk, while the cousins fell into reminiscences about childhood holidays. Brody suspected that Diarmid chose the subject specifically to exclude him. After Elspeth made a few unsuccessful attempts to draw him into the conversation, she left him alone.

At the top of the brae, they caught up with the rest of the party. This was one of Brody's favorite places on his cousin's estate. The land swept down to the turrets and battlements of the castle, with the sea and the Isle of Skye in the distance.

"I did my first Achnasheen painting here," Marina said with a nostalgic smile.

"Aye, ye took my advice about that, but no' much else," Fergus said drily, reaching across to squeeze her hand where it lay loose on the reins.

"At that stage, I was yet to discover that you're always right about everything, *caro*."

His eyes narrowed on her. "You dinnae mean that."

She batted her eyelashes theatrically. "Don't I?"

He laughed. "Ye wee besom." He turned to the rest of the group. "Anyone interested in a race? It's flat as far as the cliff, so we'll have a braw run." He raised his voice for the children to hear. "Ye bairns go first."

The suggestion received an enthusiastic response. As the youngest members of the party galloped away, Diarmid edged his horse toward the front, ready for the next round.

"Do you want to race?" Elspeth asked Brody, when he didn't move.

"Och, no." He shook his head. "I want to be alone with ye."

She frowned in disapproval. "It doesn't feel like it. You seem out of sorts."

Since Diarmid had shifted out of earshot, Brody wasn't nearly as grumpy as he had been. Usually he was accounted an easygoing companion. These recent mood swings left him bewildered and edgy. "I dinnae like ye going off with Diarmid," he muttered.

"He's my cousin."

"I ken that. But he's got a way with the ladies. Cannae imagine why. He's a damned dull dog. Always doing the right thing."

"I thought you were friends."

"If he keeps making sheep's eyes at ye, I'll friend him into a bloody nose."

Her eyes rounded, and she turned in the sidesaddle to study him. "My goodness, Brody. Don't tell me you're jealous."

Brody never blushed, so that couldn't possibly be a blush heating his cheeks. "Did he try and kiss ye?"

She still regarded him as though he'd lost his mind. Perhaps he had. If love meant a lad's sanity disintegrated, he could now tell Fergus that he was in love.

"That's none of your business," she said coolly, in a tone that as recently as two days ago, he'd never have imagined hearing from retiring Miss Elspeth Douglas.

He caught her bridle. "Show me the view across to Skye."

"You can see Skye from here," she said with a dismissive sniff.

His jaw set in stubborn lines. "I want to see the view Diarmid showed ye."

"Rocks tell no tales," she snapped, although she kept her voice down to avoid attracting notice. "You'll find no evidence of a flirtation there."

Not that their companions paid them any attention. They were too busy urging on the shrieking children who streamed across the ridge.

"No, but I'll find a girl who needs a good kissing."

She hunched one disdainful shoulder. "I'm not sure I want to kiss you, when you're in this outlandish humor."

"Are ye challenging me, Elspeth?" he asked in a low, dangerous voice.

She arched her eyebrows. "No, I'm trying to put you in your place."

He grinned at her, suddenly, illogically happy. "Och, lassie, my place is in your arms."

"Not if you're going to stomp around like an angry bear, it's not."

He tightened his hold on her horse's bridle. "I promise no more stomping."

She focused a searching gaze on him. Something in his face must have persuaded her to relent, because a faint smile curved those lush, pink lips. "In that case, Brody, you may show me the view. I think it will be unforgettable."

He laughed aloud with elation—and a measure of relief he refused to admit—and steered their horses toward the frosty trees. "I'll make sure it is, my bonny lass."

# CHAPTER ELEVEN

*E*lspeth struggled to hide a smug smile as Brody hauled her horse through a grove of Scotch pines and out onto the hillside, where hoofprints in the snow showed how she and Diarmid had followed separate paths. If Brody caught her looking too pleased with herself, he might guess just how much she relished his astonishing jealousy.

Jealousy over her. Plain, mousy Elspeth Douglas, the family afterthought.

Last night, she'd decided that Brody's kisses were the most delicious thing that had ever happened to her. Right now, his fuming reaction to her going off with Diarmid gave those kisses some competition.

How lunatic was Brody to worry about Diarmid? Diarmid was protective of her because he was her cousin, not because he was interested in her in any romantic sense.

Brody's nettled response put paid to her mother's theory that he only pursued her because nobody more attractive was available. When he asked what she'd been up to with her cousin, the temper had all but steamed off him.

It was unworthy to gloat, but Elspeth wouldn't be human if she failed to enjoy his confusion. The irony was that if she'd remained that lovelorn ninnyhammer, he still wouldn't care a whit where she bestowed her kisses.

This flirtatious game with Brody became more intriguing by the minute.

He drew the horses up in a hollow and dismounted with the easy grace that had always left her younger self swooning in delight. The smooth, controlled power of his descent had a similar effect on the newly self-possessed Elspeth. Although she refused to swoon, because it meant she might miss what came next.

"I can't see the Cuillins," she complained, just to torment him a little more. What a little cat she was turning into.

A cat was better than a mouse, by heaven.

"Och, you've seen the Cuillins a hundred times before," he growled, stalking across to seize her by the waist. His ruthless grip turned her blood to hot syrup.

"You said you'd show me." She rested gloved hands on his broad shoulders.

He stared up into her face. Under the curling brim of his hat, the blaze in his green eyes threatened to melt every patch of snow on this mountainside. "You dinnae need to see the Cuillins, when I intend to show ye paradise."

"Brave words," she scoffed, but the tremor in her voice betrayed the desire rushing through her. "Do you have your mistletoe?"

"To hell with mistletoe." He lifted her from the saddle to set her on the snowy ground. "Kiss me,

Elspeth. You're all I've thought about since last night."

Oh, dear heaven. Not even newly self-possessed Elspeth was proof against that impassioned declaration. With a sigh of surrender, she curved her body into his and tangled her fingers in his wild mop of dark curls. The air was cold, and he was so irresistibly warm.

She brought his head down until his lips met hers. This time there was no preliminary coaxing. His mouth opened over hers, and her gasp of immediate pleasure invited his tongue into her mouth. She felt like he tried to absorb her into himself. With a choked moan, she curled closer.

He lifted his head. "Kiss me back, Elspeth."

She licked her lips. After last night she recognized the tang as the taste of Brody. He groaned and shut his eyes for a moment. Then he gathered her up and began to nip and play at her lips, sucking her lower lip into his mouth and using his teeth to set her tingling. By the time she mustered the courage to copy what he was doing, she trembled, and her legs proved as unreliable as usual.

"Aye," he muttered. "Aye, that's it, lassie."

The kisses turned into a teasing contest that set her heart racing with excitement. Every glancing touch stoked the heat between them, until he dragged her up onto her toes and took her mouth with his. This time, she met the sweep of his tongue with a flicker of her own. The thrill left her shocked, and excited and eager for more.

*More...*

More led her onto forbidden paths. Even through the fog of carnal sensation, Elspeth retained just enough connection with reality to know that this passionate kiss swept her over the edge of safety and into perilous territory indeed. Which didn't stop her from giving a faint whimper of disappointment, when she pulled back from the heated darkness of Brody's kiss.

His hands tightened, then she was free. But her knees threatened to fold beneath her, and she staggered. The cold of the snow seeped up through her half-boots as she slipped on the icy ground.

"God help me," he muttered. He caught her by the waist, saving her from a fall. When she met his fierce green eyes, she knew he meant to kiss her again.

"No, Brody," Elspeth said shakily and placed an equally shaky hand on his powerful chest.

He was wearing English riding clothes, instead of his kilt. Through black superfine, the heat of his body radiated out to warm her gloved palm. On this freezing day, the temptation to snuggle up against him and bask like a cat in front of a fire was near overwhelming.

But she wasn't quite as innocent as she'd been last night when he kissed her. To her regret, she knew that any basking promised more trouble than she was capable of handling.

"I know. We're in the middle of a snowy hillside, and most of your family is just over the brae." Brody looked sheepish and disappointed, and devilishly charming, with a lock of black hair tumbling over his forehead. Some reckless part of her wanted to beg him to kiss her again, and to Hades with consequences. "I took things too far. Next time we do this, we should be inside."

She released a choked laugh. "It would be altogether wiser if we don't do this again."

His expressive black brows contracted, and he surveyed her down that lordly nose. "You dinnae mean that."

"I should." She'd hoped he understood that their flirtation was a mere diversion, but the passion brimming in that kiss made her wonder if she needed to set out some rules. "Brody, I'm not..."

The fond smile that twisted his lips only made him more charming. She fought against the premonition that she was doomed to fall under his spell again.

No, never. What on earth was she saying? Elspeth refused to confuse a few kisses with lifelong devotion. She shuddered at the thought of changing back into that soggy creature who sighed at the merest sight of him. This Christmas, flirting with Brody was fun and a sop to vanity bruised too often and too hard. It wasn't a gateway to anything permanent.

"You're saying that you're no' setting up to become my mistress."

Flooding relief set her knees wobbling again. He did understand. "That is what I'm saying."

"I have some principles." He gave a grunt of wry amusement. "Anyway, Hamish would have my guts for garters if I seduced his sister."

"He would." She paused. "Not to mention that the sister might have a few objections of her own."

That statement was pure bravado. This far, he'd treated the attraction between them lightly. She had a grim feeling that if ever Brody went after her with real intent, she'd melt like butter in the sun. Her virtue, hitherto an unthinking pillar of her existence, wouldn't survive past the first five minutes.

He paused, as if bracing himself to say something momentous. Although she couldn't imagine what that might be. Brody Girvan didn't deal in momentous statements. Yet another reason why her daydreams of declarations of undying love had been fatuous. Brody liked to skate across the surface of life. Which made him an ideal candidate for a girl testing her wings with a man for the first time.

Or at least so Elspeth had believed, until today's kiss flared into a hunger that both frightened and intrigued her.

"There you are. Why are you two hiding over here?"

Hamish's cheerful voice sliced through the portentous atmosphere building between Elspeth and Brody the way a knife cut through rope. Brody stepped away from her and turned to face her brother. "Elspeth wanted to see the Cuillins."

Hamish cantered up to them on a fine chestnut gelding. "You can't see the Cuillins from here. You need to go up the next hill."

Elspeth plastered a smile to her face and prayed she didn't look as disheveled as she felt. "I thought my horse was lame, so we stopped to check. It turns out she's fine."

Had she ever lied to Hamish before? She didn't think so. Already Brody had a deleterious effect on her morals.

Hamish shot a meaningful and not entirely friendly glance at Brody. Oh, dear, perhaps she did look as rumpled as she feared. How embarrassing.

"Is that so?" Hamish didn't wait for a response. "Everyone's going back to the castle for mulled wine and carols from the crofters. Are you coming?"

"Of course," Brody responded with an ease that she resented, however unreasonable that might be. His smooth manner was an unpleasant reminder that romantic intrigues were bread and butter to him. Elspeth Douglas was just one more lady on a long list. There would be plenty of conquests to follow her.

When he caught her waist, she couldn't help stiffening.

"What's wrong?" he whispered.

"Nothing," she replied in a low voice, knowing she was being absurd. He didn't owe her anything, let alone eternal fidelity.

Those green eyes were searching. "Are ye sure?"

"Hamish is watching."

"Ah." He spoke more loudly. "Let me help ye onto your mount, Elspeth."

With easy strength, he tossed her into the saddle and passed her the reins. "Meet me in the library tonight," he murmured as he checked her stirrups.

Her hands curled hard on the reins. "That's not a good idea."

"No, it's no' a good idea." The brilliant smile he flashed her had her foolish heart turning cartwheels, and that annoyed her, too. "It's an *excellent* idea."

"Brody..."

He caught her gloved hand and pressed it. Those glittering eyes sought and held hers. The breath jammed in her throat, and her head swam with a thousand brazen possibilities. For an instant, he didn't look like a man who took life's finer things for granted. He looked like a man stretched to the point of agony on the rack of desire. "Please."

Her lips flattened, as she struggled to keep a grip on reality. She was reluctant to trust her instincts about Brody. After all, only a few days ago, she hadn't been sure he even knew her name. "Perhaps."

"Hurry up, you two," Hamish snapped. "It's cold as a witch's tit out here."

Elspeth at last had something other than kisses to blame for her blushes. "Hamish!"

He shrugged, unaffected by her scolding. "You've heard me say worse."

"To my regret, I have. And that's nothing for you to be proud of."

Brody bent to pick up his flat-crowned beaver hat. Oh, dear. She must have knocked it off when she kissed him. How she hoped that her fiendishly intelligent brother didn't wonder what necessitated the removal of Brody's hat. Or resulted in Brody's hair falling about his face in untidy ebony waves.

She cast a quick glance at her brother's set face and saw that her hopes were in vain. Heat stung her cheeks, as she made a great show of patting her horse.

"Let's go." Hamish's voice turned as cold as the snow that stretched all around them. Without waiting for Brody to mount, he wheeled around and cantered away. To preserve appearances, however futile the gesture, Elspeth urged her mare to follow.

# CHAPTER TWELVE

It was late when Brody saw Elspeth slip out of the hall. Apart from his, no heads turned to observe her departure. People had been coming and going all night. After dinner, the guests had split into smaller gatherings and scattered throughout the house, aiding his wicked purposes.

Because tomorrow was Christmas Eve, the children stayed up late in the hall, playing games like blind man's buff and snapdragon under the indulgent eye—and with occasional participation from—their parents. Marina sat on the couch near the fire, sketching and carrying on a desultory conversation with Lady Glen Lyon beside her. Elspeth had fiddled with a few carols at the pianoforte, then retired to an armchair with a book. Fergus, Hamish and Diarmid were in the billiards room. He had no idea where Ugolino and Giulia had disappeared to. Probably some distant corner of the castle, where they whispered sweet Italian nothings to one another.

Wherever they were, they'd have no trouble finding a sprig of mistletoe to encourage their kisses. Before the riding excursion, the whole party had spent a hilarious morning, hanging bits of the plant all over Achnasheen. Ugolino's gift had provided vast amounts of amusement and copious excuses for high jinks. Fergus had chased a laughing Marina up and down the stairs, waving a cutting, and growling like a stage villain. Charles and Donald had snatched up their wives and demonstrated an ardor that surprised Brody. He'd always dismissed both men as dry sticks.

The mayhem hadn't bypassed him. So far, he'd been lured and teased and nagged into kissing two little girls, Lady Glen Lyon, Giulia, Marina, Charity, and Prudence. Every female except Elspeth, in fact. He hadn't trusted himself to kiss his wee wren, without betraying intentions that stretched far beyond the mistletoe's authority.

All night he'd struggled against staring at Elspeth, although at any given moment, he knew to an inch where she was. If he looked at her, the hunger in his eyes would give the game away. It was bloody difficult battling the temptation to gawk at her like a starving urchin transfixed outside a baker's window.

She hadn't done much to help. Tonight the lassie looked bonnier than ever. She wore a bright yellow gown he hadn't seen before, and her hair was arranged more simply than it had been last night. The loose knot flattered her gentle features, reminding him of a Raphael Madonna.

Now, for discretion's sake, he reined in his fever of impatience and delayed ten minutes before he followed her. As he shifted, Marina glanced up, and he mimed hitting a ball with a billiard cue. She nodded and smiled and bent over her sketchbook once more.

Thank God, the corridor was empty. Laughter and shrieks of excitement echoed from the hall, but otherwise the old stone castle was quiet.

Brody reflected upon the changes these last few days had worked on him. Marriage had always seemed a distant, unappealing prospect. He'd never expected the idea of cleaving to one woman alone to whip up this lather of excitement.

Until he'd looked at Elspeth and recognized that happiness had hovered at hand for years. He'd just been too blind to see. Tomorrow he'd ask her to be his wife. Hell, he'd been on the verge of proposing on the hillside.

When he opened the library door, anticipation thundered in his blood. Anticipation and a touch of uncertainty. Would Elspeth be waiting? Or had this afternoon's passion frightened her into retreat? He couldn't blame her for shrinking from the heat that flared between them. It had shocked him, and he was far from an unsophisticated innocent.

He hadn't intended their kisses to take fire the way they had. When she was in his arms, strategy turned to ashes, and all he heeded was his clamorous craving. Once she married him, he'd show her that this powerful attraction was nothing to fear. Instead, their mutual need was cause for celebration.

The library was dimly lit, and he was glad to see that a fire blazed in the hearth. While last night's encounter had been marvelous, the temperature in the morning room had threatened to freeze his balls off.

It took him a moment to locate Elspeth. When he did, a slow, satisfied smile curved his lips.

"You surprise me, lassie. Here I was convinced ye would never shrink into the shadows again."

With a grace that made his heart leap about like a newborn lamb, she rose from the window seat.

"Shadows come in handy, when I'm doing things I shouldn't."

He shut the door behind him and crossed the room to take her hand. "You're trembling."

"It's lunatic to be nervous, I know." Huge brown eyes sought his. "You've kissed me before, but this is the first time we've made an actual assignation."

He liked the sound of that. An assignation hinted at naughty acts.

Brody forced himself to recall his honorable intentions. He needed to treat Elspeth with care. She was his friend's sister. She was a guest in his cousin's house. She was still an innocent. However much he might ache to claim her, he owed it to her to wait until his ring was on her finger.

"You're no' really afraid, are you?"

"A pleasant flurry of nerves, that's all." The humor curling her lips made him desperate to kiss her. "I trust you."

Those three words enclosed him like steel bands and stole his breath. He hadn't always been a good man, but he prayed that he proved worthy of this lovely girl with her pure, generous heart.

"I willnae let you down," he said in a gruff voice.

It sounded like a lifelong vow. He supposed it was. A precursor to vows he'd make before the minister in the not-too-distant future.

He leaned in and gave her a gentle kiss to seal his silent promise of fealty and protection. Soft lips moved beneath his, before she sighed and shifted closer to bury her hands in his hair and deepen the contact.

Arousal, swift and powerful, crashed through him. A groan of yearning escaped, as he gathered her up in his arms. Soon she met his rapacious kisses with rapacious kisses of her own. How far she'd come from the skittish innocent, who hadn't known enough to open her mouth, the first time he kissed her.

Elspeth remained an innocent, however difficult that was to remember when she pressed so close that he couldn't fit a wafer between them. When she made choked little sounds of female pleasure that rang sweeter than music in his ears. When her greedy hands stroked his face, his neck, his shoulders, his chest, his back. He felt like she tried to possess him through touch alone.

Brody, the jaded man of the world, shuddered with arousal under her exploration. He wanted her more than he'd ever wanted any of his adventurous Edinburgh ladies. With difficulty, he contained the urge to swing her onto the couch and strip away that stylish gown. Instead he pushed her back against the wall and ran his hands over her lush, rounded body.

With burgeoning delight, he discovered the sinuous curve of breast and hip, the sumptuous rump. When his fingers sank into the soft flesh of her buttocks, he gasped into her mouth. How he cursed the layers of material that kept him from touching her skin.

Knowing he shouldn't, Brody began to drag up her skirts. He waited for her to stop him, as he was sure she must. Every inch he raised the froth of silk and lawn higher felt like a victory. Until he shaped his hand over the delicious arch of her bum. Frail drawers still formed a teasing barrier, but when he kneaded one round cheek, he couldn't suppress a groan of appreciation.

Her floral, female scent was more intoxicating than a barrel of claret. Hot blood pounded in his ears and made him deaf to everything but her choked gasps of excitement. Brody caught her under the buttocks and lifted her, plastering her tight against him. He tortured himself for nothing. Much as he wanted to, he couldn't take Elspeth tonight.

When he pressed her against his aching cock, she whimpered in protest and pulled away, clutching his shoulders to stay upright. "Brody, that's wicked," she gasped.

"I know," he groaned, running his teeth down her neck and wishing to hell they were already married and he could plunge inside her.

"We must stop. It's getting...dangerous." She squirmed, which did nothing to allay his excitement, damn it. "Please...please let me go."

She was right. This heat between them threatened to take charge. He had to step back, or it would be too late. He'd never verged so near to dishonor, yet his intentions had never been so pure. "Must I?"

She wriggled again, then stopped when he gave another heartfelt groan. Dazed eyes clung to his face. In the flickering firelight, her lips were red and swollen, and her untidy coiffure now owed less to art than to the raking touch of his hands. "Am I hurting you?"

His grip on her arse hardened, as he consigned propriety to Hades. Propriety, and drawers, and honor. He hadn't planned on testing the limits of his control tonight. Which made him a fool. He should have taken a lesson from this afternoon's wild kisses. "Only because I cannae have what I want, lassie."

"I think you should put me down." She didn't sound too certain.

"I should." His hands tightened.

"Then why don't you?"

"Because I cannae bear to let you go," he admitted in a hoarse rush.

He kissed her again, a duel of tongues and lips and teeth that a short while ago would have scared her. Now her hunger met his. God almighty, when he finally got her into bed, they'd set the night alight.

Elspeth struggled free of the kiss to stare at him in wonder. "Good Lord, Brody, you sound like you mean that."

"What the hell?" He frowned. "Of course I bloody mean it."

A jubilant smile stretched those full red lips. "How splendid."

"You're gloating," he said, with a hint of resentment.

"I am." She snagged her fingers in the hair at his nape and gave a gentle tug. That shouldn't bolster his excitement, but it did. Perhaps because she touched him without a hint of hesitation. "I'm very pleased with myself indeed."

Cursing those voluminous skirts that hampered his access to her, he hitched her up until her feet dangled in the air. "I'm suffering."

Two days ago, she'd been nothing to him but Hamish's shy, bookish sister. Now the mocking look she cast him under thick, dark eyelashes sent his heart slamming to a quivering stop. "Excellent."

"Ye wee witch," he groaned. "Kiss me again."

He leaned in, lifting her against the wall and glorying in the way her thighs curled around his hips. By heaven, she was almost where he wanted her. He tilted his hips into her. Even as Elspeth kissed him as if he was the air she breathed, she gave his hair a sharper tug. The sting did nothing to quiet his pounding arousal.

Brody swung her around and settled her on the leather couch, although taking things just to the limit, but no further prolonged his agony. Better by far to let her go now.

He must like pain, because his hands shifted from that sweet rump to her breasts. Through her bodice, his thumbs teased the hard peaks of her nipples.

As he edged the dress down, he covered her décolletage with a rain of kisses. If he didn't see her soon, he'd go mad. He tasted the valley between her breasts, drinking in the heady scent of her skin, then tugged aside gown and shift to reveal one creamy white breast.

"By God, you're bonny, Elspeth," he muttered and kissed the deep pink, puckered nipple.

Her broken moan betrayed her pleasure, before she jerked under him and pushed at his shoulders. "We can't, Brody."

"I ken," he said with infinite regret, suckling that perfect peak to heighten his torment.

She cried out and buried her hands in his hair. "Stop it."

"You like it."

"Of course I do, but someone could come in."

"*Certo,* you have that right," said a mocking voice from across the room. "Someone has indeed come in."

Brody wrenched upright in horror, to find Marina watching them from beside the closed door. Even in that appalling instant, something in Brody noted that his cousin's wife didn't look too shocked to find him with Elspeth.

"Oh, blast," Elspeth muttered. As she sat up, she fumbled at her bodice. Brody stumbled off the couch and stood away from her.

Her hands were shaking so badly that she wasn't making much headway. He whipped his coat off and passed it to her. She wrapped it around her shoulders with a mumbled thanks.

"We were just—" he started.

Marina's lips twitched. "Yes, you were just. I'm not sure that a night when the house is full of people is the best time to satisfy your passion."

Elspeth was blushing like a tomato and clutching his coat as if she wanted to shrink into it and disappear. "Things went too far."

"No, they didn't," he interjected, before Marina could misinterpret that rash admission.

The abrupt switch from heat and desire to the demands of real life left him reeling. His gut clenched hard on regret and the churning remnants of arousal. Heat still pumped through him, making him feel like his skin was too small to contain his body.

"I came to warn you that Hamish is looking for both of you." Marina stretched out her hand. "I'll take you upstairs, Elspeth. A few minutes with a brush and comb, and Sandra and I will soon have you looking the thing again."

"I'm sorry, Marina." The misery in her voice made Brody want to punch the wall. He hated to see her shame as she went back to fiddling—without much effect—at her sagging bodice. "You must be disgusted."

Tolerant affection warmed Marina's laugh. "Don't be a goose, *cara*. I know how mutual attraction makes the rest of the world disappear. None better. *Per Dio*, Fergus and I can't keep our hands off one another either."

"But that's all right. You're in love," Elspeth mumbled, and Brody cast her a sharp glance. What the deuce was going through that pretty head? Whatever it was, he didn't like it.

"Well, yes," Marina said slowly, looking from Brody to Elspeth and back again.

Elspeth took an unsteady step nearer to Brody. She'd managed to cover her bosom at last. "Take your coat back, or people will wonder what's been going on."

"Aye, I suppose so," he muttered, still puzzling over what she'd said.

"I'm sorry, Brody." She shrugged out of the coat and extended it toward him with a trembling hand. "I encouraged you."

"Dinnae be a wee fool, Elspeth." He scowled at her, although what he most wanted to do was sweep her up in his arms and tell her that everything would be all right. "We were both caught up in the magic."

"You're too kind," she said, and he loathed how she shrank from him as he accepted the coat.

Devil take it. This wasn't what he wanted. Elspeth was acting as if they'd killed someone.

Although thank God Marina had come in. If she hadn't, Elspeth would be compromised by now. With the woman he wanted stretched out beneath him and her breast in his hand, he'd been ready to send good intentions to Hades.

"I'm no' bloody kind," Brody snapped.

"*Smetti subito.* We don't have time to quarrel." Marina put her arm around Elspeth's shoulders and steered her toward the door. "We'll get you tidied up, *cara*, and nobody need be any the wiser that you and Brody shared a couple of kisses."

Hell's bells, she spoke too soon. Before Marina could open the door, it swung wide to reveal Hamish. Brody's gut knotted with guilt and exasperation. One minute more, and they would have been safe.

Bright blue eyes conducted a quick survey of the room's occupants, before they slowed to take a more comprehensive look. "What on earth is going on here, Brody?"

"We all wanted a chat away from the crowd," Marina said, but it was too late to hide what had happened. Brody hadn't yet put his coat on, and he was sure his hair must reveal how Elspeth had combed her fingers through it. Worse, Elspeth shrank away from Marina, like a thief caught in the act. While her bosom was now covered, her kiss-swollen lips, tumbling mass of hair, and crushed silk gown made her appear well and truly seduced.

"Hamish, it's nothing," she stammered, wringing her hands.

Ignoring her unconvincing intervention, her brother strode into the library. Without looking, he shoved Elspeth and Marina out of the way, so he could confront Brody face to face. He bristled with outrage.

"What the hell have you done to her, you bastard?" Hamish's fists clenched at his sides. "You couldn't damn well stop yourself, could you?"

Brody stared into his friend's face, and wished he could claim the moral high ground. Instead shame coiled acrid and cold in his belly. Hamish had every right to be angry. By heaven, if Marina had interrupted them half an hour later, Elspeth's virtue would be in tatters.

"Control yourself, Hamish," Brody said.

"Control myself?" Hamish asked on a rising note. "What in hell gives you the right to say that to me?"

"Devil take ye, do what you like to me, but let your sister go to her room first." Brody shifted across to put his arm around Elspeth, who looked close to collapse. "Don't be afraid, lassie."

To his dismay, she wriggled out from underneath his arm, and her response was tart. "You're not helping."

"Elspeth..." He sent her a confused glance, then turned to Hamish, spreading his hands. "I'm sorry, old man. I got carried away."

As he caught Brody's shoulder and forced him further apart from Elspeth, Hamish's voice deepened to a caustic bass that bounced off the walls. "I'd like to carry you away to a good hiding."

"Hamish, stop it." Elspeth squeezed between the two men. "You're making a fool of yourself."

"No, you're the one who's made a fool of yourself," he snapped.

"Not if this stays between us."

"Elspeth, for the love of God..." Hamish sounded ready to explode, but after a moment, his shoulders lowered.

Brody drew a relieved breath. Hamish was still furious, but that sharp brain had taken charge of his turbulent emotions. Brody didn't want to brawl with his friend in front of Elspeth and Marina. Not to mention that a bout of fisticuffs was the surest way to bring the rest of the guests down upon them.

Her brother's rage didn't make Elspeth falter. Brody admired her courage. "Hamish, it's Christmas, we're all family and friends here, and I'm not a child anymore. A few harmless kisses with an old acquaintance aren't an unforgivable sin. You're a hypocrite if you say they are. Don't forget, you've told me plenty about what you get up to in Edinburgh and London."

Hamish had the grace to look abashed for a moment, before his temper flared again. "It's different for men. For pity's sake, Elspeth, you're my sister."

"And Brody's your friend."

Before Hamish could disavow that relationship, Brody spoke. "Hamish, leave it."

"Leave what?" Elspeth's formidable mother sailed into the room, her striking face alight with curiosity and disapproval. "What on earth is all this noise about? Explain yourself, Hamish."

"There's nothing to explain," Marina said quickly, but not quickly enough.

Hamish turned on Lady Glen Lyon. "I caught Brody seducing Elspeth."

"You liar! You did not!" Elspeth protested, before facing her mother. "Mamma, he's making a mountain out of a molehill."

"*Non è niente.* Just overflowing Christmas cheer," Marina said, although she must know by now that a scene was unavoidable. "Hamish, you're overreacting."

"I'm bloody well not." Hamish was back to looking like he was set to ignite. "I saw them both when I came in."

"When we were standing several feet apart and fully dressed," Elspeth pointed out. Brody commended her persistence.

"I wouldn't say that," Hamish retorted.

"Ye have my word that I did nothing to injure your sister's reputation," Brody said in an emphatic tone, knowing that it wasn't true and would have been even less true ten minutes later.

"What's all the commotion?" Fergus appeared in the corridor behind Lady Glen Lyon.

"Will ye shut the damned door?" Brody grated out. "Every bugger between here and Glasgow doesnae need to know our business."

Elspeth's mother bustled over to her daughter. "Elspeth, are you all right?"

Brody appreciated hearing some expression of concern for Elspeth, although his wee wren seemed more than capable of standing up for herself. As if to prove that spirit, she shook her mother's hand off her arm.

"Of course I'm all right, Mamma. As Brody said, nothing happened. There's no need for theatrics.

Let's all go back to the great hall and get on with celebrating Christmas."

"Hear, hear," Marina said, moving to shut the door at last. But it was too late. A crowd filled the room, shouting questions over each other. Through the chaos, Brody returned a blistering glare from Diarmid and decided this fracas had gone on long enough.

"Stop it, all of you," he said, with an authority he'd never managed to achieve before, even at Invermackie where he still felt like an inadequate substitute for his father.

He turned to Elspeth and caught her hand. Despite her defiant stance, she was shaking. He knew that this public exposure was a horrible ordeal for her. Only a blockhead would imagine it could be anything else. At heart, she remained shy, despite new clothes and blossoming confidence.

"Elspeth, my bonny lassie, I grant that the circumstances are no' ideal." He gentled his tone. "I'm sorry I have to do this in front of a rabble, but I'd consider it the greatest honor if ye would agree to become my wife."

Astonishment widened her big brown eyes, and the color leached from her face, leaving her as pale as new paper. His fingers tightened on hers as for one awful moment, he feared she might faint.

"Th-thank you for your proposal, Brody," she stammered, after a pause that threatened to shatter his heart. Her unblinking attention didn't waver from him. He wished he knew to Hades what she was thinking.

Brody summoned an encouraging smile and spoke in the low, soothing voice he used on a skittish horse. "We'll have the banns called on Boxing Day, and we can marry in a couple of weeks. I promise I'll be a good husband. You'll never regret saying yes."

"Oh, that's lovely," Prudence said, clasping her hands over her bosom and sending Elspeth a misty smile. Diarmid looked ready to erupt with fury. Everyone else showed various degrees of surprise and curiosity.

To Brody's consternation, Elspeth didn't look anywhere near as delighted with his proposal as her sister did.

His vague foreboding solidified, when she straightened and tugged her hand free. "I haven't said yes yet."

Brody frowned at her, not understanding her hesitation. "We must marry."

She shook her head, and a stubbornness he'd never suspected she possessed settled over her delicate features. "No, we mustn't."

"Your reputation—"

"I appreciate your noble sacrifice, Brody." Her slender throat moved as she swallowed. When she went on, her voice emerged raw but steady. "But I won't marry you."

# CHAPTER THIRTEEN

Elspeth's stomach contracted into a tiny walnut, as she watched disbelief flood Brody's face. His proposal jangled in her mind like a tuneless distortion of a thousand immature, extravagant fantasies. His visible shock made it clear that he'd never imagined that she might refuse him.

"What the devil..." When he stepped forward, she backed away on wobbly knees. She couldn't blame him for looking bewildered, given that a few minutes ago, she'd been half-naked in his arms.

"Elspeth, don't be a fool." Mamma marched up to stand beside Marina. "Brody's trying to save you from a scandal."

Her mother was always organized, always in control, always in charge. Except for right now. She, like Brody, looked completely at sea. That would have made Elspeth laugh, if the situation had been less dire, and she didn't feel as if she was about to bring up her dinner.

Elspeth squared her shoulders and told herself crying and whining would do no good. She didn't underestimate the battle on her hands.

"Why should there be a scandal?" she asked, attempting to play down the night's events.

"Because I caught you with bloody Brody." Hamish sounded like he was strangling.

"No, you didn't," she said, struggling to keep her voice steady. As she looked around the circle of people surrounding her, she saw that nobody was on her side.

Then Marina sent her a smile. Relief flooded her, as she realized one person at least wasn't ready to ring a peal over her head. That silent show of support bolstered her failing courage, so she sounded more confident when she spoke to Hamish. "You barged in when I was talking to Brody and Marina. Hardly cause for gossip, let alone anything more drastic."

"Don't give me that rot, Elspeth," Hamish snapped, glaring at her. His expression said that he wanted to give her a good shaking. "You looked like you'd been..."

Yes, she could imagine what she'd looked like. Her cheeks stung with humiliation, but she made herself raise her chin and stare her brother down.

"Hamish, I'd thank ye to speak to your sister with respect." Brody angled his body between her and her brother. She'd appreciate his protective action, if he wasn't trying to protect her into an unhappy marriage.

"You're a great one to talk about respect," Hamish retorted. "You had your filthy hands all over—"

"A few kisses at Christmas don't make me a scarlet woman, Hamish," Elspeth interjected, to break the dangerous tension rising anew between the two friends. "Anyway, we're all family here. Even if there was a small indiscretion, why should any talk reach beyond Achnasheen?"

Elspeth stifled a pang at her hypocrisy, given how close she'd come to giving herself to Brody. She might tell herself she wouldn't have let things go that far. But she hadn't intended to let him touch her bottom or breasts either, and she'd made not a whisper of a protest when he did. His hands conjured magic, and she'd been helpless to resist him.

"Elspeth, I don't understand. Are you saying you dinnae want to marry me?" Brody asked, and if she didn't know better, she might wonder if his hurt went deeper than a blow to his pride.

What nonsense. Of course it didn't.

She sucked in a breath, struggling to ignore the devastation darkening Brody's chiseled features. "No, I don't." The three words stabbed her heart. "Although I appreciate that you're trying to save my reputation."

"It's nae just that, Elspeth."

She shook her head and even summoned a smile. "You're very kind to say so."

"Elspeth, you're being a foolish, ungrateful, headstrong girl," her mother said, folding her arms over her bosom and regarding her youngest daughter with a bellicose expression. "Have a thought to your future. If you won't consider yourself, consider your family. Consider me. I have a role of great influence in this country. How will anyone in politics respect me if I can't control my own daughter?"

Oh, no, this was getting worse and worse. If her mother got far enough up on her high horse, she would be immovable. Elspeth cursed the recklessness that had created this mess, although even now, some wicked, female part of her couldn't regret the kisses.

"*La povera ragazza.*" Marina spoke before Mamma's harangue could proceed past the point of the unforgivable. "How can Elspeth make a decision, with everyone glaring at her as if she's committed murder? As she says, a few kisses at Christmas aren't a mortal sin. There's no need for all these bitter recriminations. Lady Glen Lyon, I know I'm not family, but why don't you leave me alone with her for a wee while?"

"No, I need to talk to Elspeth on my own," Brody said, his tone dogged.

Diarmid shoved his way through the crowd in the doorway, his impressive jaw stuck in a belligerent jut. "By God, that's the last thing we want."

This far, Brody had kept control of his temper, so Elspeth was surprised at his flaring anger as he turned on her cousin. "You stay out of this, ye interfering bastard."

"I wish to hell you'd kept out of this and far away from her."

"What Elspeth and I do is no concern of yours."

Two large, powerful males faced up to one another. Fear joined the wild turmoil of emotions already churning in Elspeth's stomach. If anyone she loved was hurt as a result of her misbehavior, she'd never forgive herself.

"She's my cousin, and I willnae stand by and watch a rake debauch her," her cousin growled.

"Diarmid!" Elspeth protested. "Will you listen to me? Nobody has debauched anyone. You're letting your imagination run away with you."

"And your bloody mouth as well," Brody said, still squaring up as if preparing to throw a punch.

"Stop it, both of ye." Fergus stepped in between the two men. "All this huffing and puffing isn't helping."

"You're wrong there," Diarmid said stiffly. "Pounding this bugger into the ground would help me a lot."

Brody's lip curled in a sneer. "I'd like to see ye try."

"I wouldn't," Marina insisted.

"Nor would I," Elspeth said.

"Elspeth you're too young to realize what this lout is capable of," Diarmid said, without looking at her.

"Diarmid, stop it. Brody's your friend, and he deserves better from you. You've said quite enough, even though I appreciate your defense of my virtue." Which wasn't entirely true. She was biting back the impulse to clout her cousin. Not only was he making a bad situation worse, but he hovered close to calling her a mouse. She'd rather be seen as a loose woman than the nonentity she used to be.

"Elspeth—" he began, but she spoke over him, tired of the battle of male egos, tired of the accusing looks, just...tired.

"I think you've all said quite enough." To her surprise, she didn't sound like she was about to scream.

"You cannae—" Brody wasn't giving up.

Nor was she. "Right now, I'd like all of you to leave me alone. I've said I won't marry Brody. No harm's been done." Except to her heart, and she just had to live with that. "The matter's at an end."

"Far from it," Hamish objected. "You mightn't care for your good name, but I do."

"Then stop acting like a buffle-headed idiot and making such a ridiculous scene," Elspeth snapped back.

Her hard-won composure was disintegrating. She couldn't take much more of this—she'd spent her life avoiding conflict; shouting always made her feel sick—but if she showed the slightest sign of weakness, the family would fall on her like jackals attacking a wounded antelope. They'd insist that she accept Brody as her husband and as she weakened under the pressure, she might fall in with their plans. That meant disaster.

"Unless you marry Brody, you'll be a pariah," her mother said, in a portentous voice that sent foreboding oozing down her backbone.

"But, Mamma, nothing happened," she said, knowing that her mother had gone past the point of listening. "You're overreacting."

"Overreacting, am I?" Her mother's lips tightened in self-righteous anger. "See if you feel the same when you no longer have a home to come to."

The buzz of whispers in the room faded to nothing, and everyone turned in shock to Lady Glen Lyon. Elspeth's mother's face was set like stone and indicated that cannons wouldn't shift her on this issue.

"Are you threatening to disown me, Mamma?" Elspeth asked, appalled and incredulous. How on earth had everything come to this?

"*Per pietà*, I don't see why you should take things that far, Lady Glen Lyon." Marina once more put an arm around Elspeth's shoulders. "I promise you that when I came in, I saw nothing beyond a little harmless flirtation."

"Then why was Hamish so exercised about what he discovered?"

Mamma had the bit between her teeth. She might relent in time but right now, she was determined on making her position clear. She'd see that everyone suffered the torments of the damned before she stepped back from her ultimatum. If she stepped back.

Elspeth wanted to retort that Hamish had been in a rage because he was an idiot. But that wasn't fair.

"He misunderstood," she said, knowing she was wasting her time.

"Lady Glen Lyon, your daughter is as pure as a lily," Brody said. "Ye have my word as a gentleman."

"That's all very well, Brody, but appearances are what count. I have my political influence to worry about," her mother said. She directed an implacable stare into the space above Elspeth's head as if she couldn't bear to look at her erring daughter.

Elspeth blinked back stinging tears. Tonight had been wonderful—up until it wasn't. One of the saddest parts of this quarrel was that over the last few days, she'd hoped that she and her mother had grown closer. She should have known better.

If her mother imagined that bullying would change Elspeth's mind about marrying Brody, her mother didn't know her at all. Once Elspeth made her mind up, nothing would shift her. Look at her ill-fated penchant for that handsome rogue Brody Girvan.

She'd inherited that strong will from her mother. If Mamma really decided to turn her back on her daughter, she'd cut Elspeth loose from the family. Her stomach had been roiling since Marina had come in. Now she raised a shaking hand to her lips and prayed that she wouldn't be sick. That would be the final beastly humiliation.

"Elspeth, listen to me. Dinnae get your hackles up. If ye do, you'll never listen to sense," Brody said. "This issue is between you and me. Please say you'll marry me."

She gave him credit for injecting such desperation into his voice. She also had to give him credit for knowing her well enough to understand that beneath her unassuming exterior, she possessed a formidable obstinacy. It seemed her mother didn't know her half so well.

"It's not just between you two, though, is it?" Hamish said. "Elspeth's ruin is a family matter."

Brody shot him a furious glare. "If you dinnae shut your mouth this minute, I'll shut it for ye." His fists clenched at his sides, and the threat of incipient violence vibrated in the air once more.

"This is my house, and I willnae have it turning into a bear's den," Fergus said sternly.

"Elspeth, please?" Brody turned back to her with a pleading expression that almost made her wonder if refusing him was the biggest mistake she'd ever made in her short life.

Oh, dear Lord, he sounded like he cared about her, and she knew he didn't. Everything would be different if he did.

She braced to answer as she must. "No, Brody. I said I won't marry you, and I'm standing by that."

Her mother gave a furious huff and whirled toward the door. "Then you're dead to me, Elspeth."

"I won't be coerced, Mamma," Elspeth said, fighting the urge to run after her mother and beg her to reconsider.

"You know she won't, Mamma. She's like a mule when she gets her mind stuck on something," Charity chipped in. "You're going about this all the wrong way."

Her mother stopped but didn't turn around. "She'll listen when she starts to wonder where she'll sleep tonight."

"Elspeth has a home here as long as she likes," Marina said in an uncompromising tone that to Elspeth's surprise matched the strength of her mother's. "She's not a child. She's almost twenty-one. She has a right to wed where she wishes."

Elspeth wanted to hug her, while relief as powerful as a tidal wave swamped her. "Thank you, Marina," she mumbled.

Marina's kindness undermined her show of strength. She felt closer to crying now than she'd felt since Hamish had come in.

Fergus glanced at Hamish, Diarmid and Brody and must have decided that they'd retreated from the brink of a brawl. Hamish and Diarmid looked disgruntled, but in control of their impulses. Brody, blast him, still looked desolate as if all his hopes had crumbled to nothing. She didn't believe that was true for a minute.

"I dinnae think there's anything to gain from continuing with this tonight," Fergus said. "Why don't we all go to bed? In the morning, I doubt circumstances will seem as desperate as they're painted right now."

"The voice of common sense, *il mio tesoro*." Marina bestowed an approving smile on her husband. "*Per l'amore di dio*, nothing good can come of this atmosphere of grand drama. Let's all settle down and wait for tempers to cool. We can decide our next actions then."

Brody folded his arms over his chest and his jaw hardened in an adamant line. "I'd like to talk to Elspeth before she goes upstairs."

"So ye can bully her into accepting you?" Diarmid asked snidely.

"As if I'll let you put your paws on my sister again," Hamish snarled, tensing up once more and bunching his hands at his sides.

"Hamish and Diarmid, you can both stop it right this minute," Elspeth said. When she'd kissed Brody, she'd felt brave and free. Right now, she felt dirty and shabby and discarded. "For the tenth time, I didn't do anything wrong."

Her brother directed a fulminating glare at her, before he shot Brody a look of pure hatred. "No, *you* didn't."

The atmosphere, calmed thanks to Marina's good sense, flared toward conflict again. Brody looked angry and hunted—and hurt in a way she hadn't expected.

She did owe him some explanation, she supposed. But not now. At this moment, she felt too close to breaking.

"Brody, can I please talk to you tomorrow?" To her chagrin, her voice cracked. "Tonight, I'm—"

"Over my dead body," Hamish shouted.

"Stop bellowing like a maddened elephant, Hamish." She directed a quelling look at her brother. "If I want to talk to Brody, I will."

"I'm the head of the family."

She narrowed her eyes. "That's all well and good, but given Mamma just disowned me, I'd say your authority is at an end."

"*Brava, ragazza,*" Marina said, coming forward with a managing air. "I grow tired of all this noisy masculine posturing."

"Let me posture and clear the room for ye, my love," Fergus said. He addressed the crowd with the unmistakable authority of the Laird of Achnasheen. "Go to bed, everyone. This will all seem like a silly tiff tomorrow."

The autocratic tone worked. With some grumbling, the room emptied of everyone but Fergus, Marina, Elspeth—and to her dismay, Brody.

"Elspeth, we can't leave things as they are right now," he said stubbornly.

She crossed her arms, feeling harried to the point of shrieking. Would this horrible night never end? "You just want to propose again."

"At least I'd like to ken why ye said no." She hated that he sounded kind and reasonable, and as if he had a right to question her decision.

She clenched her shaking hands in her skirts. "We wouldn't suit."

"But—"

"It's late, cuz. Too late in the day to start all this up again." Fergus strode across and clapped him on the back. "Come and have a wee dram in the drawing room. You look like ye need it."

Instead of shifting, Brody stared at Elspeth, as if he strove to pierce through her skin to discover the secrets lurking in her heart. She hoped to heaven he didn't succeed. There were a few secrets there she had no intention of sharing with him—ever.

"I'll ask again, Elspeth," he said with grim emphasis.

Close to despair, she shook her head and turned away from that penetrating gaze. "My answer won't change."

"Leave her be for tonight, Brody." Marina's arm tightened around Elspeth's shoulders. "Can't you see she's at the end of her tether?"

"Thank you, Marina," Elspeth whispered.

"Very well. But this isn't over," Brody said, his tone grim, even as he and Fergus headed for the library door.

After the door closed behind the cousins, leaving Elspeth alone with Marina, she sucked in her first full breath in forever. Nausea still soured her stomach, and she felt bruised and unsteady, as if she'd been crushed under a runaway carriage. "I'm sorry. I seem to have ruined your Christmas party."

Marina shrugged as she released her. "*Cavolo*, don't you get all operatic on me, Elspeth. This isn't such a big problem. Anyway, a little scandal enlivens a dull winter."

"It doesn't feel like a little scandal," Elspeth said in a low voice. Marina's calm acceptance of what had happened helped her feel less like a worm.

Marina surveyed her, black eyes perceptive and, more importantly, kind. "I'm sure it doesn't."

"If you hadn't come in—"

"Pfft." Her airy gesture was unmistakably Continental. "You have too much sense to lose your maidenhead to Brody Girvan on the library couch. Anyone could have walked in."

Marina's levelheadedness started to shrink the grand tragedy to manageable proportions. "Anyone did walk in."

"Exactly."

Elspeth looked away and twined trembling hands together over her heaving stomach. "I didn't feel sensible when Brody kissed me."

Marina's laugh held a note of wry fondness. "We never feel sensible when we're in love."

Elspeth made a choked sound and raised shocked eyes to her friend's face. "I never said I was in love."

Marina rolled her eyes with such theatricality that at another time, Elspeth would have laughed. "You didn't have to. As long as I've known you, you've never had a thought for anyone else."

Elspeth had imagined that she'd finished blushing for the night. Marina's accusation dashed those hopes. She strove to sound as if the idea was insane. "Oh, I might have harbored a girlish *tendre* for him, but I've grown out of that."

"Is that right?" Marina asked in carefully neutral tones.

"Of course." With manufactured casualness, Elspeth imitated her hostess's characteristic shrug. "I came to realize that he'd never look at me as anything but Hamish's boring little sister. You reach a stage where you need to accept there's no point crying for the moon."

Marina still studied her with the same concentration she devoted to a complicated drawing. "Yet tonight, the moon came very close to you, *bambina*."

It had. Damn Brody. Any closer, and she'd really be ruined instead of just accused of it. "It was just a bit of flirtation."

"Flirtation can signify a more serious interest. The handsome young laird has spent the last few days following you with his eyes. It's a pity that you've outgrown your interest in him, just as he's grown into an interest in you."

"I'm the only unattached female at this party." Elspeth couldn't quite contain her bitterness, as she pointed out the unassailable fact.

"Oh, Elspeth," Marina sighed, with a humiliating mixture of impatience and sympathy.

Elspeth bristled. "It's true."

"Yes, it is. But that's not why he's enchanted. Don't you know you're lovely?"

"Because you fixed up how I look," she insisted.

Marina continued to study Elspeth with her perceptive artist's eyes. Eyes that saw too much, including the falsehood of her claims of indifference to the Laird of Invermackie. Another prickling flush mottled Elspeth's cheeks, but she leveled her shoulders and raised her chin, ready to counter any well-meant arguments.

But Marina only released a soft, "Ah."

"You understand," Elspeth said in relief.

"*Certo*." Marina's eyes were still kind. "You fear that this new, polished version of Elspeth Douglas has blinded him to what you're like under the primping."

Feeling awkward, she sidled from foot to foot. Perhaps she'd have done better to go to bed when everyone else had. This conversation was almost as difficult as the horrible scene that preceded it. "Yes," she mumbled. "He never looked at me before."

"I don't think he was ready to see you until now."

"I'm still the same unadventurous creature I ever was."

"Not really." Marina's lips twitched. "*Per pietà*, that girl would never have sneaked away in the middle of a family party to kiss a rake."

Despite everything, Elspeth gave a choked laugh. "No, that's true."

She resisted pointing out that no self-respecting rake would have been caught dead kissing the frump she'd been, either.

Marina took her hand. "I meant what I said about staying here. I won't have you coerced into a decision you don't want to make."

Elspeth squeezed her fingers. "I appreciate that." She pulled away. She feared Marina's kindness. Already tonight, it had threatened to bring her tears to the surface. She was afraid that once she started crying, she'd never stop. "Mamma will get over it. Sooner rather than later, if we're lucky. She'll realize there's no reason for gossip to spread beyond the family and affect her precious political influence. It's all just a storm in a teacup."

Right now, the night's events didn't feel like that. Brody's proposal, when he spoke the words she'd longed to hear for so many years, still felt like the worst moment in her life.

"If she doesn't forgive you, remember you have friends."

Elspeth mustered a shaky smile for this woman, who was generous enough to champion her. "Thank you."

"Now I think you want to be alone to have a good cry." Marina's voice developed a practical note. "Time for bed."

"You're too good to me."

Another Continental sound expressing dismissal. "I like you."

"I like you, too," she said huskily.

"I'm glad, *bambina.*" Marina kissed her cheek and squeezed her shoulder in reassurance. "Now try and sleep. There's nothing more to be done tonight. Fretting never did anyone any good."

Elspeth felt as wrung out as an old dishcloth, but despite her exhaustion, she knew a night of fretting was inevitable. She summoned another smile, even shakier than the last. "Who would have thought that the family would throw me out on my ear for licentious behavior?"

"*Si*, who knew?" Marina released a soft huff of laughter. "I suspect you still have the capacity to surprise all of us."

"I surprised everyone tonight," she said, in a voice thick with unshed tears. She couldn't help remembering her mother's coldness, and Hamish's rage, and Brody's brave attempt to save her from scandal. That had been the most difficult of all to bear.

"That's not necessarily such a terrible thing, *cara*. Now, go to bed. Tomorrow is Christmas Eve. A day of transformation and hope."

"I don't feel very Christmassy," she admitted.

If she could, she'd run away from her family and her duty and every mistake she'd made. She'd escape from the horrid memory of Brody's unconvincing proposal, and even worse his unconcealed astonishment when she said no. His astonishment and more upsetting, his hurt.

Most of all, she wanted to escape the knowledge that everything she'd done and said during the last few days turned out to be a pack of pathetic lies. She'd decided she would no longer love Brody Girvan. She'd believed that she could dabble in a flirtation, without risking her heart or her honor.

Tonight's fiasco proved both predictions tragically false.

"Let's see what the morning brings." Marina watched her, still with that understanding expression softening her dark eyes. "I'll walk you to your room and fight off anyone who might lie in wait."

Elspeth's response was closer to a sob than a laugh. "I couldn't bear another scolding."

"No scoldings, *ragazza*. Not tonight. My word as a Scotswoman. Even if I'm a Scotswoman only by adoption."

# CHAPTER FOURTEEN

After that turbulent scene in the library, Brody didn't sleep a wink. He hadn't suffered a restless night over a female since those adolescent days when he'd been head over heels in love with Polly Macrae. If a week ago, someone had told him that the next woman to torment his nights would be Hamish's mousy sister, he'd have laughed in their face.

By God, he wasn't laughing now.

In fact, as he came downstairs in the dark, with the hope of catching Elspeth at breakfast, he had the strangest conviction that his sole chance of happiness depended on persuading this stubborn, unusual, gorgeous girl that she must marry him. Even more lowering for a man credited as a devil with the ladies, he was far from convinced that he would prevail.

As he'd expected and despite the early hour, Elspeth sat alone in the morning room, staring into a cup of tea with a disconsolate expression. A slice of toast sat untouched on a plate near her elbow. Brody paused in the doorway and took stock of what he saw, struggling to work out the best approach.

The lassie looked deathly sad. How else would she look? Because he'd been a selfish blockhead all his life, he'd lured her to take risks with her good name. Now she was exiled from her family and reviled as a light skirt. Last night, he'd burned to protect her from attack. She'd rejected his every effort as too little, too late.

Devil take her, it was worse than that. She'd rejected him.

Her terse denial still stung like acid. He'd never asked a woman to marry him before. When he did, he'd never imagined his choice would have the temerity to say no. While he'd been angry last night, beneath his anger, he'd been hurt. And shocked—which said far too much about his conceit.

The unbelievable had happened. Elspeth had refused to marry him. Not all the haranguing and blandishments in the world had shifted her from that decision. He'd spent all night, not just regretting her response, but examining his soul. And finding it sadly wanting.

Until these last months, he hadn't been much in the habit of self-reflection. Like most young men of acceptable manners and appearance, not to mention large fortune, he received a warm welcome wherever he went. He'd never found any particular reason to question the general opinion that Brody Girvan was a fine fellow.

But he'd had an unhappy year. Finding the woman he wanted had made him hope that his life might start heading in the right direction. But it turned out that woman didn't want him.

Once he'd left Fergus, he'd stood at his bedroom window, staring out over the snowy hills of Achnasheen, and facing up to the unwelcome truth that Brody Girvan wasn't such a fine fellow after all.

He was selfish, and self-indulgent, and inclined to believe the world was ordered purely for his pleasure. Most people who met him never probed far enough beneath his debonair shell to discover the darker elements. Yet now he knew that his three closest friends harbored doubts about his character. Hamish, Diarmid and Fergus believed that while he might make a braw companion for a night's carousing, he wasn't worthy of Elspeth's hand.

That had hurt, but not as much as Elspeth Douglas had hurt him, when those assessing brown eyes had penetrated through to the vacuum in his soul. She'd been adamant that she wouldn't have him as her husband, even if the marriage restored her good name and her place in her family.

Yet while he knew that she was better off without him, Brody couldn't stop wanting her. He'd never longed for anyone the way he longed for Elspeth, while she'd decided he didn't deserve her time or affection.

Desolation and self-hatred left a cold, rusty taste on his tongue, as he now surveyed the woman who had brought him to his knees. The view wasn't encouraging.

She'd dragged her hair back from her face in the familiar, severe style—no seductive tumble of mahogany curls today. She wore an old brown dress that Marina mustn't have thought worth altering. It was plain that his wee wren had decided that she wanted to sink back into the shadows where she was safe.

But it was too late for her to hide away. Brody had seen her flaring beauty. He'd seen it, even before she decided to share it with the world. Elspeth Douglas would never again fade into the background, no matter how she tortured her hair or buttoned her collars up to her stubborn chin.

He sucked in a broken breath, nervous as a schoolboy approaching his first love, and stepped through the door. When she raised heavy eyes to observe him, the lack of welcome in her expression might daunt a laddie less determined.

The lamplight revealed signs of crying. Her pink eyelids and woebegone features made him sick with guilt. He'd set out to make this bonny girl happy, and all he'd done was cause her grief.

"Good morning, Elspeth," he said in a somber voice.

"Good morning, Brody," she said no more brightly. Looking hunted, she stood up when he dared to venture closer. "You're early this morning."

"No' as early as you."

"I had trouble sleeping."

He already knew that because of the purple shadows under her eyes. "So did I."

"I'm sorry to hear that," she said, edging out from behind the table. "Enjoy your breakfast. I'll see you later."

He didn't shift to let her past. "I need to talk to ye."

Her slender white hands performed a nervous dance in the air. "I'd rather leave you to eat in peace."

"Thanks to you, I haven't known a moment's peace since I got to Achnasheen," he said grimly. "I'm here because I knew this is the one chance I'll have to get ye alone."

Something that looked like panic crossed Elspeth's face, and she retreated a shaky step. "This is an ambush."

He frowned, not sure what he could do to make her listen. "Aye, if ye like."

She squared her shoulders and took up a belligerent stance familiar from last night, when she'd been intransigent about not wanting to marry him. He was in such a low state that this felt like an improvement. Her defiance was preferable to her fear. "I don't like."

"Too bad." He gestured for her to sit down again. "I willnae take much of your time. Ye owe me that much."

She leveled a hostile glare at him from under lowered eyebrows a darker brown than her luxuriant hair. He wondered whether she would insist on going. If she did, what could he do? Tying her to the chair was unlikely to promote his cause.

To his relief, she released an annoyed sigh and sank back into her chair.

"Thank you." Brody crossed to the sideboard. "Would ye like some coffee?"

Her hands curled around the arms of her chair, and her answer was snappish. "I'd like you to say whatever you feel you need to, so that I can go back to my bedroom."

"And hide?"

"Don't I have reason?"

"I dinnae think so." He brought two cups back to the table, although she hadn't said she wanted one. "What we did wasnae that bad."

"Mamma thinks it was."

He sat down opposite her. "If you dinnae mind my saying so, Lady Glen Lyon seemed to enjoy the theatrics of it all."

To his surprise, the corners of her lips deepened in a ghost of a smile. He'd wondered if she'd ever smile at him again. "I don't mind you saying so at all. It's true. I'm hoping this morning, that she's thought better of banishing me from the Douglas fold. I suspect she'll sulk for a couple of days and cast a pall over everyone's Christmas, before she decides that things aren't as dire as she thought."

"She sounded pretty convincing when she disowned ye."

"Yes. But as you say, our crime wasn't so heinous. Given any scandal will stay within the family and only Marina saw the worst of it, I'm sure Mamma will come to terms with a scarlet woman for a daughter."

He gave a grunt of disagreement. "You're no' a scarlet woman."

"No, I'm not. I'm a fool."

The bitter little admission revived his scowl. "What in Hades does that mean?"

She slid the fresh cup of coffee in front of her and stared down at it with the same discontentment she'd directed at her tea. "It means I should have known better than to think I could have a brief and harmless flirtation with a handsome man, without suffering any nasty consequences."

Brody inhaled through his teeth, as the sting in her comment found its target. "Are ye saying marrying me counts as a nasty consequence?"

Slowly she raised her eyes to study him. "Aren't you?"

"No, by heaven, I'm not. I want to marry ye."

The smile that twisted her lips astonished him, and made him feel sick to the stomach. It was calm and jaded and utterly joyless. "That's gallant of you, Brody."

"For God's sake, lassie, I'm nae being gallant. I mean it."

Her eyebrows rose at his fervor. "Then you're not thinking straight. We'd be terrible together."

"We weren't terrible when we kissed."

"That's because you're very good at kissing." She'd been pale when he came in, but now a faint pink tinged her cheeks, reminding him of the rosy, passionate creature in his arms last night. "It's not because of anything I did."

"You show great promise for a beginner." More than promise. Her burgeoning passion had sent him up in flames. God help him when she got a bit of expertise under her belt.

"Thank you, but a few kisses are no basis for a lifetime together."

Despite the fraught moment, her prim response made him smile. "Och, we have more than that."

"No, we don't," Elspeth said, with a bleak finality that made his heart shrivel to the size of a pebble.

"I like ye." He knew the moment called for a stronger declaration, but under that steady brown gaze, his courage failed him.

"I like you, too. But I don't want to be the woman you're forced to marry."

"I'd planned to ask ye to marry me before last night."

For a moment, Brody wondered if his confession might sway her. The brief spark in her eyes faded, and she shook her head with a weary tolerance that made him want to smash his cousin's expensive porcelain breakfast service to dust. "You're being kind again."

"No, I'm not. It's true."

How the hell was he making such a mull of this? He'd always thought he had a way with the lassies. Elspeth had liked him enough to kiss him. Why the deuce didn't she like him enough to marry him?

"Then thank you," she murmured.

"Does that mean you'll say yes?" he asked without much hope.

"No, it doesn't. We have nothing in common. I'm a quiet little mouse, and you're a sophisticated man of the world. I'd bore you to tears before the ink dried on the marriage lines. Don't be fooled by Marina and Sandra's handiwork. I'm still Hamish's dull little sister."

"I never thought of ye that way."

More bitterness twisted her lips. "You never thought of me at all."

Perhaps there was some truth in that. But couldn't she see that he'd changed? Only now as he noted her closed expression did he truly accept that he'd failed. She wasn't going to be his.

And he'd never wanted anything more.

His large hands closed into fists on the polished mahogany table. "Are you trying to say I'm no' good enough for ye?"

Her eyes widened. "Brody..."

He could no longer bear to sit still and pretend this was a polite discussion and not the end of every dream he'd built around her during the last days. When he surged to his feet, he shoved the chair back hard enough to send it toppling over with a thud.

"You're right. I'm not good enough." His voice was rough with the force of his emotion. "But if ye marry me, I swear I'll do my damnedest to make myself worthy of you."

She looked startled. "I'm...I'm flattered."

He made a sweeping gesture of dismissal. "I dinnae want you to be bloody flattered. I want ye to say you'll marry me."

That stubborn line returned to her chin, although he could swear he saw genuine distress in her eyes. He supposed she wouldn't like hurting him. "I can't say that."

"Aye, you can."

"In that case, I won't." With a shaking hand, she refolded the white linen napkin she'd laid beside her plate and stood up. "Please..." Her audible inhalation was the first real sign of vulnerability she'd betrayed. "Please leave it at that, Brody."

A thousand furious, passionate arguments massed in his throat, but he swallowed them back. They tasted like poison. Last night, he'd accused her family of bullying her, yet now he came close to doing the same. Every second confirmed that he wasn't worthy of her, and the knowledge threatened to tear his heart to ragged shreds.

"Aye, very well," he said stiffly, stepping back. He offered her a formal bow, as though they were strangers, and he'd never kissed her, or laughed with her, or nurtured the hope that she might be the woman to lend his ramshackle existence weight and purpose. "Under the circumstances, I wish ye farewell, Miss Douglas."

Brody didn't wait for Elspeth to respond. Instead, he turned on his heel and marched out the door, wondering what the hell he was going to do with the rest of his useless life.

# CHAPTER FIFTEEN

"Here you are. I've had a devil of a time finding you."

At Hamish's impatient exclamation, Elspeth looked up from where she huddled on the window seat in the library. Given this was the scene of her humiliation last night, she supposed it was a strange place to seek refuge after that excruciating encounter with Brody at breakfast. But from the moment she'd discovered what books were, she'd found comfort and pleasure—and, yes, sanctuary—in their company.

"That was the idea." Despite her best efforts, her voice was scratchy with the tears she'd shed in the last couple of hours, since Brody had given her that chilly bow and stalked off in a huff. Refusing him was the right thing to do. She knew it in her bones. If only that made her feel better. "What do you want, Hamish?"

"I've come to apologize." He had the grace to look a little shamefaced. "I flew off the handle last night."

"You did. If you'd managed to keep your mouth shut, we could have avoided all the drama." She bent her head and brushed shaking hands over her wet cheeks. "How is Mamma?"

"I don't know. She hasn't come downstairs yet."

Given her mother's love of an audience, that spoke volumes about the scale of her current sulk. "So she hasn't forgiven me."

Soon the reality of Elspeth's banishment from the family would sink its claws into her heart. Right now, she was still struggling to cope with making such a mess of everything with Brody. The wider consequences of her ruin hadn't yet impinged on her wretchedness.

"You know how important her political influence is to her."

"More important than her daughter's happiness," Elspeth said, before she could help herself.

She waited for Hamish to accuse her of disloyalty and lose his temper again. Her brother's emotions tended toward the volcanic, although given time, he'd calm down enough to see reason. Look at his apology now for blundering in on her last night.

Hamish didn't respond with his usual heat. Instead he studied her with the sharp perception that somehow muddled along beside his mercurial temper. He was intimidatingly clever—people in scientific circles spoke of him as the next Astronomer Royal. But he didn't always choose to focus that titanic brain on petty earthly concerns, instead of on the vast universe over his head.

"Perhaps she thought a match with Brody Girvan would promote her daughter's happiness."

Humiliation prompted another prickling blush. "I suppose everyone in the family has guessed that I was mad about him," she said in a sour tone.

"Aye, we did. That's why we're flabbergasted that you turned down his proposal."

She scrambled to her feet, shoving aside the Maria Edgeworth she hadn't been reading. "He doesn't want me."

Hamish's eyebrows rose, so he looked like a skeptical Viking. "Didn't seem that way to me."

"He didn't mean anything more than a bit of nonsense at Christmastime. It would be cruel to make him pay for a small indiscretion with a lifetime of unhappiness. Until I changed my hair and my clothes, he didn't know I existed."

Hamish frowned, as he winnowed through what she'd said. "That's not true."

Elspeth's laugh was unamused. "Don't try and butter me up now, Hamish. You never have before."

"I could swear..." He crossed to stand before the blazing fire. "He asked my permission to court you."

Shock flooded her, and she subsided onto the window seat again as her dratted knees collapsed beneath her. Brody had told her that he was trying to woo her, but she hadn't believed him. Had she got everything wrong? "C-court me?"

Hamish glanced up and spoke with certainty. "Yes, he'd decided that he wanted to marry you before all that brouhaha last night."

She still had difficulty crediting that he'd considered her as a wife. Not to mention that courting wasn't an activity she associated with rakish Brody Girvan. It seemed too staid for such a Lothario. "What did you tell him?"

"That he's not good enough for you." His expression hardened. "It's not for me to tell tales out of school—"

Despite her confusion, a scornful laugh escaped Elspeth. "You tell tales out of school all the time. How else do you think I know what a roué Brody is?"

Her brother looked uncomfortable. "Diarmid might have—"

"Diarmid's as silent as the grave when it comes to gossip, and you know it."

"Aye, he is." As usual when he lost the argument, Hamish shifted his ground. "It's a good thing you know about Brody. I won't have my sister marrying a libertine."

"Did you refuse him permission to approach me?"

It was Hamish's turn to express contemptuous amusement. "I told him I had bugger-all influence over you and that you'd make up your own mind. People who don't know you mistake your quietness for malleability, whereas you're as stubborn as a mule when you set your mind on something." His dark gold brows drew together again, as he considered the situation. "So I don't understand why you won't marry Brody. You decided you wanted him years ago, and you've never wavered. The fellow proposes, against all the odds, and you take some imp into your mind and say no. I'll never understand the female of the species. Give me a constellation any day."

Elspeth still reeled to learn that Brody had asked Hamish for her hand. Were all those passionate kisses meant to serve as the prelude to a proposal, and not just a way to pass the time when he was bored? "Why didn't you say something about this last night?"

Hamish's rocklike jaw tensed. "I thought the bastard was trying to force the issue by compromising you."

"We wouldn't have gone so far," she said, mortifyingly aware that she wasn't sure about that at all.

Hamish didn't look too convinced either. "Brody's got a way with the ladies. You haven't seen how he works when he's got seduction in mind. He's unstoppable."

She didn't want to think about that—although at least he'd never wanted to marry any of his previous inamoratas. While it seemed that he just might want to marry her. "I thought he was your friend."

"He is, but damn it, you're my sister. I don't want you hurt."

"Thank you." With every minute, her grudge against her brother became harder to maintain. She could guess what that declaration of allegiance cost him. While Hamish wasn't demonstrative, Elspeth knew he loved his family, including her. "Brody's not a bad man. I think he's just a bit wild. And his father's death threw him out of step."

Hamish regarded her with dawning wonder. "Damn me, you're still in love with him."

Her blush had faded. Now it flared anew. "I've outgrown my childish hero worship."

"Yes, you have," he said, but spoiled it by going on. "Now you're really in love. Until death do you part. Forever and ever. Amen."

The urge to deny her brother's statement welled, but jammed unspoken behind her teeth. She turned away to hide her terrible secret, although now it was no secret to Hamish.

"Of course I am," she mumbled, twining her trembling hands together in her lap.

What was the point of denying the truth? She'd always loved Brody. She had a sick feeling in her stomach that she always would. Her decision to forsake her penchant for him was nothing but pique and pride and hot air.

She could no more stop loving Brody than she could stop having brown eyes. He was part of her, whether he loved her back or not.

"God give me strength," Hamish bit out in angry bafflement. "Then why in hell won't you marry the cove?"

Since last night, Elspeth must have shed enough tears to fill the loch outside. Surely there were none left to cry. Nonetheless hot moisture pricked her eyes, and she raised unsteady hands to dash it away.

"Because he doesn't love me," she said in a choked voice.

"Are you sure?" Hamish left the hearth and stepped closer. "Last night, when you refused him, he looked like you'd shot his dog. And Fergus and his kin are very fond of their dogs."

"Even if he does think he loves me..." Although she couldn't imagine he did. She gulped down a sob. "It's because I'm dressing better, and wearing my hair differently, and—"

"And speaking up, and lifting your head out of your book now and again, and showing that there's a woman of spirit under your shyness." He paused and subjected her to a thoughtful inspection. "In fact, you haven't been shy at all this Christmas."

"It's not the real me."

"Of course it is." Hamish was annoyed again. She couldn't blame him. Even in her own ears, she sounded addled. "If your new dresses made Brody notice you, all well and good. He was never going to fall in love with someone who spent her life scuttling around the edges of the room like a wee mouse."

Elspeth bit back a groan. The mouse word again. She cast her brother a look of renewed dislike. "He only started paying attention after Marina put me in Sandra's hands."

"Does that matter, as long as he pays attention?"

"Yes, it does," she insisted, even as she wondered if her pride was condemning her to a lifetime of loneliness.

"I'll say it again. I'll never understand women," Hamish said, rolling his eyes in masculine disgust. "You're saying that you've finally got what you always wanted, but you're not going to take it, because you can't accept that the man you love thinks you're pretty?"

"That's not fair, Hamish," she said in a raw voice. "He wants to marry an imposter."

"No, he doesn't." Hamish was still frowning, as if prodding his massive brain to shift away from cosmic issues to concentrate on merely human ones. "He asked my permission to court you before you turned into the Belle of Achnasheen. It was three days after he arrived, when everyone still thought you were a shy wee sparrow. He spoke to me just before you came downstairs and dazzled us. I'll lay money that I'm right about the timing."

Through her fog of misery, Elspeth wasn't sure she'd heard him right. It seemed too good to be true—too good and too awful, because since then, she'd done her level best to wreck her chances with Brody Girvan. Saying no to his proposal last night and again this morning had come close to killing her. In fact, this morning it had been even worse because, while logic insisted that his deeper feelings weren't involved, she couldn't mistake his genuine chagrin at her refusal.

She turned to survey her brother, wondering if he ran mad. Or if she did. "Say that again," she said slowly.

"Brody asked permission to court you on his third night here, just after Ugolino and Giulia turned up, and before you came downstairs in your new dress." Hamish didn't seem to realize that he changed her entire world with just a few words. In her turmoil, she didn't even mind that he spoke to her as though he addressed someone of weak mind. "You could have knocked me over with a feather when he did. I'd never thought he was smart enough to notice what a hidden treasure you are."

Her brother's uncharacteristic compliment passed her by. "He asked you for my hand before he saw me in my new clothes?"

Hamish gave an irritable grunt. "Didn't I just say so?"

"Yes, you did."

"I can't see that it matters much when he asked."

After such misery, joy struck with painful force. "It does matter."

"Women!" her brother bit out. "Now you're crying again, when for a moment there you looked almost happy. What the devil's set you off now?"

She sniffed, as she fumbled in her pocket for her handkerchief. "I'm happy."

"Good," Hamish said, eyeing her doubtfully and passing her a pristine square of white linen. She was in such a state that she'd failed to locate hers.

Elspeth blew her nose and forced her mind to work past the astonishing truth that Brody had meant it when he said he wanted to marry her. Her,

Elspeth Douglas, not some painted doll Marina and Sandra had created between them.

"I need to see Brody. Do you know where he is?"

"I think he's gone back to Invermackie," Hamish said as if it didn't matter.

Her heart, which had begun to dance with a mixture of excitement and hope, dipped into plodding despair again. She lurched to her feet. "He's gone?"

"I think after what happened last night, he decided he was no longer welcome."

"But it's Christmas Eve."

"I doubt he was feeling very festive."

"Oh, no." She had so much to make up for. "How long ago did you see him?"

Hamish shrugged, and she could tell that his tolerance for feminine ups and downs faded fast. "I don't know. An hour maybe."

"You didn't try and hit him again?" she asked in horror.

"No, I bloody didn't." Hamish started to look seriously grumpy. "He had the grace to apologize for what happened last night."

"He hadn't done anything wrong."

"He had, but he'd also done his best to fix it. Not that his chivalry did him an ounce of good. You refused him anyway."

"I'm not refusing him now," she said, clutching at her skirts. "If I run, I might catch him before he goes."

"And what if you don't?"

"If I don't, I'm going to ride after him." Determination rang in her voice. "All the way to Invermackie, if I have to."

"What?" Hamish's crankiness vanished in amazement—and displeasure. "Elspeth, what the hell has got into you? Come back here!"

But she'd rushed past him. Skirts flying, she dashed down the corridor toward the stables.

# CHAPTER SIXTEEN

Elspeth wasn't dressed for the outdoors, but she couldn't bear to wait to change into warmer clothes. Cold as well as desperation added speed to her mad skitter across the icy yard, swept clean of snow, to Fergus's luxurious stables.

"Jock, have you seen Brody?" she asked the brawny Scotsman who was grooming Fergus's gray mare Banshee.

The pause before the Highlander spoke threatened to split her heart in two. She braced to hear the news that Brody had already set out for home. "Aye, lassie. He's in the back, getting ready to head off. Although I told him it's daft to set out alone on a snowy day like this. And no Christian should leave his family on Christmas Eve."

"I agree." A dizzying wave of relief made her clutch at the edge of the stall. Thank heaven, she wasn't too late to offer amends to Brody. Nor did she need to make good on her vow to Hamish to gallop over the wintry hills in pursuit of the man she loved.

"Brody!" she called, rushing along the aisle dividing the stables. "Brody, where are you?"

"Devil take ye, what's the matter?" He stuck a tousled dark head out of the last stall. "Stop caterwauling, lassie. You're frightening the horses."

He wasn't being funny. Nervous whinnies from high-bred stock marked her noisy, frantic progress. Because of the Christmas house party, the stables were packed with expensive horseflesh.

She'd pictured flinging herself into Brody's arms and declaring without ceremony that she'd be his wife. But his bleak expression and unwelcoming tone had her stumbling to a halt outside the stall. This wasn't the man who had swept her up to heaven in the library last night, but someone sterner and warier.

He'd hung his coat over the gate, leaving him free to work in his shirtsleeves. Her eyes drank in the sight of that large, powerful chest clad in loose white linen, while crippling shyness trapped her joyful acceptance unspoken in her throat.

"What are ye doing here, Elspeth?" he asked in a flat tone she'd never heard him use before.

She'd imagined he'd be pleased to see her, but the green eyes were flatter than his voice. She shivered and wrapped her arms around her torso, although a line of braziers kept the stables toasty warm.

"Hamish said you were leaving." Elspeth despised her uncertain tone. She'd hoped that over the last few days, she'd developed a bit of backbone, but she was back to sounding like mousy Miss Douglas.

He shrugged and returned to strapping his baggage to the saddle. "There's no point staying. And it's pretty clear that most of the party would welcome my absence."

"I wouldn't," she found the nerve to say, edging into the stall and standing just behind him, although something about the tense set of those impressive shoulders warned her against touching him.

He gave a rough tug to the strap fastening his valise. "Ye more than anyone."

She wanted to argue, but she knew he wouldn't believe her. "It's Christmas Eve. You can't leave."

"Aye, I damn well can," he said through his teeth, still without looking at her.

"But you'll be on your own at Christmas."

"I need to get used to being alone."

She winced. "Why?"

His shoulders, broad and straight, heaved with a great sigh that expressed endless irritation. "Why in hell do ye think?"

She twisted her fingers together and blinked back more tears. It had been a cursed watery kind of day. Summoning every scrap of courage, she raised her chin and told herself she could do this. What Hamish had told her suggested that Brody's feelings might be involved at a deeper level than mere male vanity. She prayed her brother was right, or she was about to make an awful fool of herself.

"Please don't go, Brody."

"God almighty," he muttered savagely and whipped around to glare at her. "Don't ye understand yet, Elspeth? I want you. I want ye more than a dying man wants his next breath. Because I cannae have you, it hurts. I'm nae fit company right now."

She gasped, appalled at the corrosive unhappiness in his eyes. Biting her lip hard enough to draw blood, she made herself meet that blazing gaze without flinching.

As she studied him and read his seething anguish, astonishment as well as remorse stabbed her. How on earth had ordinary little Elspeth

Douglas inspired this storm of passion in rakish, sophisticated Brody Girvan?

"You can," she said, her voice so low she hardly heard the words herself.

He jerked up to his full, imposing height and scowled down at her. "What are ye up to, Elspeth?"

She struggled for a little more conviction. "I said you can have me."

A silence bristling with anger and confusion and, yes, longing crashed down between them like an avalanche. Brody's bay gelding whickered and shifted, picking up the tension thrumming between the two humans who shared the narrow stall with him.

Brody sighed again, although this time with regret rather than anger. The belligerence drained from his face, and that tall, strong body sagged as he ran his hand through his black curls, leaving them even untidier than they'd been when she came in. Which was saying something. He looked like he'd spent the day tearing at his hair.

"Elspeth, sweetheart, there's no need to be afraid. You don't have to give yourself to a man ye dinnae want, just to make sure you've got a roof over your head. Marina and Fergus will let you stay, and I'm sure your mother will forgive ye." He sounded kind and reasonable and, to her chagrin, distant. "I suspect she's halfway there already. After all, we only kissed. You're as pure as ever you were."

His determination to mistake her meaning made her want to stamp her foot. Although she supposed given the emphatic way she'd refused him—twice—she couldn't really blame him for missing the point. "Why on earth are you so obtuse, Brody?"

Confusion made him grimace. "Obtuse?"

"Yes, obtuse." At least she'd stopped squeaking, although quarreling with the man she loved didn't strike her as a great improvement. "I'm trying to tell you that I'll marry you."

There, she'd said it. As plain as day. She waited for him to seize her and kiss her the way he had last night.

Instead, he crossed his arms over his chest and surveyed her down that haughty nose as if she were a clumsy housemaid who'd spilled dirty water over his best boots. "There's no need to panic about your future. I said your mother will come round."

"I'm not panicking," she retorted, clenching her fists at her sides. "I thought you'd be glad that I've accepted your proposal."

"Only if you want to marry me."

She gave a growl of frustration. "What about all that stuff you just said? That you want me and you can't live without me?"

"What about it?"

"I'm here to tell you that you've got me."

"Have I?" He tilted a skeptical eyebrow. "Or have I only got the chance to restore your good name?"

"Last night that's what you tried to do."

"Aye, well, that was last night." Another heavy sigh escaped him. "I've since decided I dinnae want a dutiful bride, who marries me for convention's sake alone."

"I promise you I won't be dutiful." When her small joke sparked no amusement, she spread her hands in bewilderment. "Brody, a mere couple of hours ago, you proposed to me again."

"And ye refused me in no uncertain terms."

Elspeth felt like giving him a good shake. Couldn't he see that none of that mattered anymore and she was his for the taking? "So this is about pique?"

His mouth turned down. "No. Yes. Maybe." He rested his large, elegant hand on his horse's glossy bay withers, and his tone sharpened. "What do ye want, Elspeth? There's only a few hours of daylight left, and I'd rather no' be riding across the hills after dark."

He'd proclaimed he wanted her and despite his irascible temper right now, she believed him. It shouldn't be this hard for her to speak up.

"You." Elspeth fought to steady her quaking voice, recognizing she had a fight ahead to get him to trust her again. "I want you."

For a moment, she wondered if that was enough. Something bright sparked in his eyes, turned them glowing emerald. Then to her regret, it faded, and he looked as moodily handsome and unhappy as ever. "You need to spell it out, lassie. I thought you wanted me last night, and we all know how my conceit brought me down."

"I want you, and I'd love to be your wife," she mumbled.

"What did you say? I didn't hear you."

Resentment coiled in her belly, along with the more familiar longing and uncertainty. It made her feel braver. "Now you're just playing with me."

"Maybe," Brody said sourly. "You've been playing with me since the day I arrived at Achnasheen." Anger roughened his voice as he went on. "What in hell did ye mean by kissing me like that, if you didnae mean to have me?"

A huff of incredulous laughter escaped, although she remained a long way from amused. "I can't believe I'm hearing this! You're the blasted libertine. Did the country miss toy with the rake's affections and lead him up the garden path about her intentions?"

Her sarcasm made anger tighten the skin of his face, giving her a sudden glimpse of what he'd look like when he was old. "Well may ye mock. Even I can see the absurdity of it. But nonetheless it's true. You led me on, Elspeth. You made me think that your feelings were engaged when they weren't."

Guilt cracked her defiance and jabbed her like a hundred needles. How she'd hurt him. She'd had no idea.

"They were engaged, Brody," she admitted, meeting his gaze with an unwavering stare. It became clear that nothing but unconditional surrender would break through the carapace of injured pride—and feelings—he'd built around himself.

"Then why did ye refuse me?"

Before she confessed that, she needed to be sure of him. She almost was, but not quite. "Why did you ask me? Was it just to save my good name?"

Brody ran his hand through his hair again, and she read an unfamiliar defenselessness in his face. "That was part of it."

She licked her lips. What a fool she'd been to imagine that luring Brody back would be easy. "But not the sole reason?"

The hand on the horse's withers tightened into a fist. "No, not the sole reason."

Her confidence rose a fraction. "And did you flirt with me because you were bored?"

"Of course not." He looked offended. "I flirted with ye because I couldn't resist you."

That sounded even more encouraging. Elspeth took a faltering step closer. "And you didn't kiss me because Marina made me look pretty?"

"You've always been pretty. Marina just made it easier for the world to see what was already there."

"I didn't think you'd noticed me before."

He sighed again. "It's hard to explain, at least without confirming that I'm the careless numskull that ye already think me."

"Try."

The helpless gesture was new, as was the air of defeat that hung about him. "I've been a wild young man. There's no point lying about that."

"No."

For the first time, genuine, if bleak humor lightened his expression. "Hamish and his blasted big mouth."

"Yes."

"But during this last year, I've just been going through the motions. Playing the libertine has become more work than it's worth. I've felt aimless and useless and lost."

"I'm sorry." She knew without him telling her, that he'd never confided his unhappiness to anyone else.

"There I was, sick of the world, sick of myself, and most of all, sick of my deuced self-pity, when I turned up at Achnasheen to spend Christmas with people I've known most of my life."

"No high expectations that anything special might happen?"

"None at all. But then I saw ye. I dinnae think I'd ever seen you before. No' properly."

"What...what did you see?" she dared to ask, inching even closer.

His faint smile warmed in a way that made her heart jump around like a grasshopper. A powerful surge of hope stole her breath. After all the confusion and pain, she and Brody might yet have their happy ending.

"An interesting lassie, who didn't seem too impressed with me, a sure sign of intelligence. A lassie who hovered in the shadows while the rest of her family monopolized the sunlight. A sweet, pure-hearted lassie with no idea how beautiful she is."

"Oh, dear," Elspeth said, her voice catching on a husky note. "No wonder the Edinburgh ladies were mad for you. You shouldn't say such things if you don't mean them."

Irritation at her continuing lack of faith tightened his features. "Damn it, I do mean them." He sucked in a breath and spoke more calmly. "But that day, what I saw clearest of all was that I was nowhere near worthy of this exquisite creature."

She swallowed to shift the jagged boulder of emotion blocking her throat. "That didn't stop you from kissing me."

He shrugged. "I'm only human, my darling."

The endearment threatened to undo her. Surely now he'd kiss her again. Instead he turned back to his horse and began to unbuckle the bag he'd just attached to his saddle.

"What are you doing?" she asked in bewilderment.

"I'm no' going anywhere today." Brody set the valise on the ground.

She swallowed again. "I'm glad."

"Are you?" he said, still facing toward his horse.

"Yes." She sucked in an uneven breath and steeled herself for his answer to the question she must ask. Although after what he'd just said, she wasn't as nervous as she had been. "Brody, leave your saddle and horse and straps alone for a moment and look at me."

With slow deliberation, he did, his green eyes so dark and deep that they belied his claim to being a shallow man. But of course, he wasn't half as shallow as he pretended to be. He never had been.

"Please stop skirting around the truth. Tell me why you proposed."

She expected him to revert once more to avoidance or annoyance, but instead his shoulders slumped. Brave, shining Brody Girvan looked vulnerable as she'd never before seen him.

"Och, *mo chridhe*," he said, in that beautiful baritone brogue that always made her want to melt into a puddle of delight at his feet. "That's easy to answer. I asked ye to marry me because I love you."

# CHAPTER SEVENTEEN

*B*rody watched shock flood Elspeth's features, shock and disbelief. No immediate pleasure, he was devastated to note. He could see that his declaration didn't alter her feelings for him.

With a grim precision of movement, he went back to unsaddling Perseus. This frustrating, painful conversation meant he'd lost any chance of reaching the next inn before the winter night fell. While he might be desperate to get away, he wasn't mean enough to inflict a freezing journey on Perseus.

"Is that...is that it?" she asked unsteadily from behind him. "'I love you, Elspeth,' then it's back to life as usual?"

He didn't turn around. An acrid brew of desire, misery, and futile yearning churned in his belly. If he looked into her eyes, he didn't trust himself not to grab her, even though he knew she didn't return his love.

"There is no life as usual since ye turned my world upside down." He shifted to unbuckle the bridle, patting Perseus when he'd finished. The horse whickered and bumped his noble head against

Brody's shoulder. "Good boy. I'll wager you're delighted we're no' going anywhere."

"So am I," Elspeth said in a small voice.

Because Brody couldn't imagine she meant that, he didn't answer as he pushed past her to fetch a bin of oats. He took his time. He hoped that when he came back, she'd be gone. Having her close, yet out of reach, was agony.

Elspeth was waiting for him. Along with a revival of her militant mood. Her arms crossed over her lush bosom, and her eyebrows lowered in reproof. "Brody, I know looking after your horse is important, but do you think you could stand still long enough to talk to me?"

"We've been talking. Last night. This morning. Now." He filled Perseus's manger and patted the glossy bay neck again as the horse buried his nose in the oats. "It hasnae done me a wee ounce of good."

"I wouldn't say that," she said softly.

This time, something in her tone pierced his thick veil of unhappiness, and he did at last give her his full attention. By God, looking at her hurt. It hurt like hell. It was a bitter reminder of everything he wanted but would never have.

"I told ye I loved you." He cursed the hint of surliness in his voice.

"Yes, you did." He couldn't read her expression, but her stance hinted that she was torn between running, or staying to battle it out. At least she wasn't looking quite so much like William Wallace addressing his troops before they mounted a raid on the invading Sassenachs.

One thing was certain. She didn't look like a girl who had discovered that her love was returned.

She bit her lip. "Did you mean it?"

Brody stifled an angry response. After all, his bad reputation with the lassies was nobody's fault but his own. She had no particular reason to trust him, even if he wished to Hades she did. "Aye."

Something changed in her brown eyes, although her expression remained wary. So he was surprised when she reached out to take his hand. Wee Elspeth rarely initiated contact, although when he held her in his arms, she followed his lead with breathtaking alacrity.

Her touch shuddered through him like a gunshot, jolting his aching heart into an unsteady jog. Being with her when she didn't love him was excruciating. He began to wish he'd ignored her and headed out into the snow when he had the chance.

"Come over here and talk to me," she murmured. "I'm sick of fighting Perseus for your attention."

"You're playing with fire, lassie." His lips flattened, although he didn't try to pull away. Pride told him to send her to the devil, but he didn't listen to it. This might be the last time Elspeth held his hand. He'd be damned if he cut the contact short. "I'm an inch away from flinging ye over my saddle and kidnapping you away to Invermackie."

He'd expected that to spark outrage, but to his surprise, she laughed. At the sweet sound, the turmoil in his soul eased to a mere storm, instead of a hurricane that promised to devastate everything within reach. "I might like that."

What on earth? That almost sounded promising. "Would ye?" he asked on a skeptical note.

She squeezed his fingers. "Perhaps you can try it, after I've talked to you."

The last twenty-four hours had left Brody too battered for optimism, but nonetheless, a cautious hope began to sprout inside him. That tentative hope and his curiosity kept him cooperative as she led him across to a bale of hay in an alcove near the tack room.

Elspeth sat and drew him down beside her. He hardly dared speak for fear that this fragile truce might shatter.

How the mighty had fallen. Before he fell in love with Elspeth, he'd never been uncertain with the lassies. But then, no other woman had mattered to him the way his wee wren did. One false move, and she'd flutter away forever.

For the first time since that fraught scene in the library, he started to wonder if the situation was as irreparable as he'd believed. By now, he'd expected to be well on the way across the hills, cold outside and in. A broken heart chilled a man's blood. Yet he was still here, because she'd asked him not to go. Now she held his hand in her lap and idly played with it as if she had every right to touch him.

At the other end of the stables, Jock whistled as he worked, while this hidden corner offered a haven of privacy. On most days, the stables bustled with activity, but on this snowy Christmas Eve, his cousin had given the grooms a holiday.

Brody waited for her to make good on her promise to talk to him, but she seemed content to sit near him and hold his hand. The suspense reached such a pitch, he could no longer stay silent. "Elspeth lassie, if you've brought me here just to let me down again, I'd rather be out in the snow with only the wind for company."

She stared down at his hand in hers, her expression pensive. With painful longing, his gaze fixed on her delicate profile. How bonny she was. The bonniest girl he'd ever seen. He must have been blind not to realize that Hamish's quiet wee sister was a jewel awaiting discovery.

"I need to make a confession," she said softly.

"Oh?"

"More an explanation, than a confession." Still she didn't look at him, although she licked her lips, betraying her uncertainty.

He bit back a groan. What he wanted to do was seize her in his arms, and kiss her into a swoon. Then he'd tell her to stop tormenting him and admit she was his.

A week ago, even yesterday, he might have swept aside her hesitation and done just that. But he'd learned a lot about her—and himself—since last night's row in the library. A show of passion might sway Elspeth into temporary surrender, but if he wanted lasting capitulation, he needed to step back and let her come to him on her own terms.

Brody wasn't by nature a patient man, but for Elspeth, he could wait. Hell, now she'd given him a glimmer of hope, when all hope had been dead, he'd wait until Doomsday if he had to.

When he didn't say anything, she went on in a low, steady voice. "It's about a very silly fifteen-year-old girl, who set her sights on an unattainable young man."

"Not that unattainable," he couldn't help saying.

He received an admonitory glance for his trouble. "Please don't interrupt."

Brody hid a smile. Which was surprising, too. When he'd saddled Perseus, he'd been convinced he'd never smile again. "I beg your pardon, my liege."

"Granted." Her lips twitched.

"Go on with your story." He hoped to God that it didn't end with the silly girl growing up and deciding that her interest in the young man was nothing more than a childish infatuation.

"This silly girl pined in vain, because it was clear that she was never going to attract the young man's eye." She gave him another quelling glance when he shifted in protest. "She was shy and bookish and frumpy, and nobody saw her as special, not even her family. The young man never noticed her, or how much she was in love with him."

The word "love" snagged on his heart like a fish hook. "Elspeth—"

"He wasn't to blame." She pressed on before he could set her right on that unflattering description. "The girl was so tongue-tied in his presence, that she could hardly force out a word."

"She's fixed that particular problem," Brody couldn't help pointing out.

"She has." She cradled his hand in hers with a tenderness that he prayed wasn't the prelude to a final farewell. "For five years, the girl yearned after the boy in silence, living for the few occasions when she saw him. While the boy grew handsomer and handsomer and spread his charm far and wide."

Aye, he'd done that, all right. To his shame. Discomfort made him shift again, but this time, he was smart enough not to speak.

"He spent his time chasing beautiful girls from all over Scotland, and didn't spare a moment's attention for the girl who loved him best of all."

This was sounding better and better. His heart leaped into life.

"Then just before Christmas the year she turned twenty, the girl saw the error of her ways. Her handsome laddie was never going to love her. The truth was inescapable. She could wallow in impossible dreams that made her miserable, or she could be sensible and stop loving him."

"Blast you, Elspeth," he growled, ripping his hand from hers and staring at her in consternation.

"Are ye putting me through all this just to refuse me again?"

At last, she turned to face him, her rich brown eyes searching. "I haven't reached the end of the story."

"I'm no' liking the direction it's taking."

"Stay with me, Brody." Her eyelashes fluttered down again. "From now on, the handsome laird would be nothing more to her than her brother's friend. She made a vow that she'd no longer yearn from the shadows."

"Deuced good thing ye did," he said grumpily. "Talking to me was a great way to catch my notice."

Wry amusement deepened the corners of her lips. "She'd decided she no longer wanted the young man to notice her. Remember—she'd renounced her love."

He gave an impatient sigh. "The young man did notice ye."

"Yes, he did." She kept staring down into her lap. "But by this stage, the girl looked rather different, thanks to a clever friend. When the young man wanted to flirt with her, she was flattered enough to succumb to a few kisses. Especially now she was immune to any deeper feelings."

"For pity's sake, Elspeth..."

At her raised hand, he fell silent once more. "After he'd ignored her all those years, she wanted to see how it felt when a rake pursued her."

"What was it like?"

"Oh, it was wonderful." This time she did look at him, and the melting expression in her coffee-colored eyes revived the hope that withered when she said she renounced her love. "He was a very good kisser, and he made her laugh. She felt like such an attractive, sophisticated lassie, to have this wild boy in her thrall, just for her own pleasure and not with any view to forever."

"Speak for yourself."

Elspeth ignored that. "However, this delightful interlude came to a nasty end when their harmless flirtation became public knowledge."

"Nasty?" Every muscle in his body tensed. She'd used the word before. He hadn't liked it then. He didn't like it now. "You mean my proposal?"

"Yes," she said, taking his hand again. If she damn well meant to send him on his way, she shouldn't touch him. But he couldn't resist curling his fingers around hers. "The rake turned out to be a man of honor, and he asked the shy girl to marry him because he thought he'd compromised her reputation."

"And she told him no." That wound still ached.

"She couldn't see why a little Christmas cheer should decide their whole future."

"It decided mine," he said flatly.

She squeezed his hand. "She knew the young man had singled her out because she was the lone unattached lady in the party, and even then, only because her clever friend had changed the way she looked."

He shot her a furious look. "You must ken that's not true."

"I do now."

"Elspeth—"

"Please let me finish."

"Very well." He clung to her hand the way a drowning man clutched at a piece of driftwood, trying to snatch one more breath before he went under.

In the distance, he heard Jock lead Fergus's horse out to the yard. He and Elspeth were now alone in the vast stables, with only equine witnesses to whether the next few minutes ended in heartbreak, or life with the woman he loved.

"It was even worse than that." For the first time, her steady calmness faltered.

"How could it be worse?" he muttered.

Her mouth turned down. "It was worse because the girl had been lying to herself the whole time."

"Had she?"

"Yes. It turned out love isn't that easy to banish, after all."

His pulse starting to race, he sat up straight and stared into her face. "It's not?"

She shook her head. "No. She'd told herself that what she felt for the handsome lad was puppy love."

"It wasn't?"

"No. Our heroine was really in love."

Elspeth loved him? Was that what she was saying? She was going about all this in such a roundabout way, he still wasn't sure.

"*Mo chridhe...*" He reached for her, but she released his hand and stood up.

"Brody, I need to tell you this." She held her hand out in appeal. "You asked me last night why I said no to your proposal."

The temptation to catch her up against him was nigh overwhelming. He lowered his arms and forced himself to stay patient. After all they'd been through, he knew better than to bully her into doing what he wanted. Even with kisses. And she still hadn't said the words he ached to hear, however close she verged to them.

"So why the devil did you refuse me?" Her story left him more baffled than he'd been before he'd heard it. "Seems a boneheaded thing to do, if I want you and you want me."

"I thought you were only indulging in some idle amusement, before you go back to your usual entertainments."

He surveyed her with incredulous disfavor. "Because I can't resist my habit of flirting, even for a couple of days, and ye were the only candidate? Although you dinnae meet my usual standards, I was so desperate, I'd have to make do?"

She winced at his sarcasm, and a pretty flush colored her cheeks. "It sounds absurd when you say it like that."

"Aye, it sounds absurd, because it is." He sighed and stretched his legs out across the wooden floor. "And to think everyone tells me you're clever."

Her gaze dug down into his soul. Before he fell in love with Elspeth, he'd never given his soul much thought. Now he hoped to hell that she didn't find it as wanting as he feared.

"Brody, I'm not clever about you," she said in a muted voice. "I never have been. I'm sorry I was so mean to you at breakfast."

He hid a shudder. "You werenae too bad—if ye wanted a man to leave you in a rush to cut his throat."

She grimaced and took a step closer. "I didn't know you cared then."

"I care," he said in a low voice. "More than I've ever cared for anything in my worthless, self-indulgent life."

She studied him, as if she discerned hidden depths in him nobody else ever had. "Hamish says you cared before Marina made me look pretty."

"Good God, Elspeth, is that what all this is about? I told you—you were bonny, even before ye spruced yourself up."

She touched her severe hair. "Didn't you like it?"

An unamused huff of laughter escaped him. "Only because the rest of the world saw you, too. I didn't need the competition."

The tension leached from her expression, and warmth softened her brown eyes. She sat beside him again and took his hand. "Oh, Brody, that's lovely."

He stared at her in frustration. She'd held him off long enough. Especially now he was sure—or almost—that she loved him. "It would be even lovelier if you put me out of my misery and tell me you love me."

She looked startled. "But I did."

"Only in passing, and only in terms that made you sound ashamed of how ye feel."

She raised his hand and kissed his knuckles. The brief touch of her lips shuddered through him and made his heart crash against his ribs in a tempest of longing. "I love you, Brody."

He'd pretty much bullied her into saying it, but the words he'd ached to hear carved an Elspeth-shaped hole inside him. "You do?"

"I've always loved you." Her smile was shaky, and she stared into his eyes with a shy sincerity that reminded him of the girl he'd first met. "The miracle is that I think you might just love me back."

The weight of failure and misery that had dogged him all day began to lift. He stood and drew her up to face him. "If ye think anything else, you're not the canny lassie I credit you to be."

"I haven't felt too canny over the last few days." Those large, glowing eyes examined his face, and for the first time, he read the light as love. At last, invincible hope unfurled inside him like a banner of victory.

Brody tightened his grip on her hand and angled in to kiss her. When her lips fluttered against his, he restrained the urge to deepen the kiss. They'd always had desire, but right now, words alone had the power to bring them together. As he drew away, she made a faint sound of complaint.

"I love you, lassie," he murmured.

The first time he'd told her, she hadn't believed him, not really. With every repetition, he saw acceptance seep into her skin, settle in her bones, claim a place in her valiant heart. By the time they'd spent fifty years together and he'd told her ten thousand times, his love would be an indelible part of her.

"I love you, Brody," she replied, with a tender fervor that banished the last of his unhappiness. Not just over the last few days, but the difficult months before. He knew now he'd been restless for a good reason. He'd outgrown the pursuits of his youth, and had started to seek a lifelong purpose.

In Elspeth, he'd found that purpose. Gratitude turned his tone reverent. "How I've longed to hear ye say that."

A faint frown crossed her face. "Why didn't you tell me you loved me last night?"

He grimaced. "In front of that crowd—and with ye looking like your world had ended?"

"My world had ended." Her mouth twisted in a wry smile. "I'd just realized that I was still in love with a man who would never care for me, yet who felt honor-bound to shackle us together for life. I couldn't imagine a surer recipe for a wretched future."

"Is that still how ye feel?"

The smile changed, became a sensual invitation. "If you kiss me again, I might answer that."

He smiled back. "Not yet, *mo chridhe*. I intend to do things right this time around. On the previous occasion when I tried this, I made an utter shambles of it." He dropped to one knee on the wooden floor beneath him.

"Brody…" she whispered, clutching at his hand. Her eyes rounded, and color tinged her slanted cheekbones as she stared down at him.

He struggled to shift the emotion damming his throat. This shouldn't be difficult. After all, she loved him and he loved her. But the words were too important to emerge easily. "Elspeth Douglas, I love ye with all my heart, and while I'm nowhere near good enough for you…"

She shifted as if to disagree, but he went on before she could interrupt. "While I'm nowhere near good enough for you, my sole hope of happiness is to have you by my side for the rest of our lives together. Through good times and bad. Through the years, when I'll strive with all my power to be a fine husband. Say you'll marry me, Elspeth, because I'm lost without ye."

Tears brightened her lovely eyes, even as delight illuminated her delicate features. She looked a different creature from the woebegone girl at breakfast.

When she didn't respond straightaway, he tightened his hold on her hand. "This is my third proposal, my darling. Please say yes this time."

Her throat moved as she swallowed, and her voice emerged in a husky whisper. "Oh, Brody, you make me so happy. This morning, I thought I'd never be happy again."

He stared into her face, recognizing her as his destiny. "I'll do my best to make ye happy for the rest of your life."

Her lips curled in a smile that expressed a universe of joy. For the first time, he genuinely believed that she did love him. "I'd love that."

"I love you."

"And I love you."

"So?"

She laughed, and the warm sound rippled down his backbone and settled in his heart. "Of course I'll marry you, Brody."

Once she'd declared her love, he'd known she'd have him, but hearing the words shifted the final traces of uncertainty that had weighed on his heart like an anvil.

"Oh, my beloved," he sighed and brought her hands to his lips. "Thank you. I'll never let ye down. I swear it."

"Now I'm convinced you should kiss me, Brody."

Overwhelming emotion making him clumsy, he struggled to his feet. He lashed his arms around her and drew her against him, glorying in the soft lushness of her body and how she welcomed his touch. "Aye, I recall that last time we were rudely interrupted."

"We might be rudely interrupted this time, too," she said, so incandescent with elation, she shone like a thousand stars.

As Brody stared down into her vivid face, he didn't feel triumphant. Instead he felt blessed.

He'd never imagined having the power to make anyone feel like this. It was a responsibility, and one he intended to live up to as long as he drew breath. His grip on her waist tightened. "When you're my wife, I'll have ye to myself."

"I'd marry you tomorrow." A spark of the delicious humor he'd discovered in the last few days lit her eyes. "Well, perhaps not tomorrow. It's Christmas Day."

"What a rare Christmas gift fate has delivered into my hands." He smiled back at her. "And we're in luck, sweetheart. Marina has hung that unimpressive Sassenach weed all over the castle. So as long as we're standing under it, I can kiss ye whenever I like."

Elspeth gave a cracked laugh and buried her fingers in his hair. "Stop talking, Brody."

He stared down at her, dazzled with happiness, dazzled with her. "But don't ye—"

His shy wee beloved gave his hair a sharp tug. Even as he winced, she rose on her toes and dragged his head down for a kiss that wasn't shy at all.

# EPILOGUE

*E*lspeth rested in Brody's powerful arms as Perseus ambled toward the small building under the brow of the hill, picking his way across the firm snow on his neat black hooves.

"Are ye tired?" Brody murmured, guiding the bay into the shadowy stables at the back of the isolated hunting lodge, deep in the hills behind Achnasheen Castle.

Elspeth made a drowsy sound and rubbed her cheek on Brody's shoulder. The wool of the plaid he'd flung over his shoulder was soft beneath her face. She drew in a deep breath redolent of hay and horses, and the delicious scent of the man she'd married. "A little. Mostly just happy."

He didn't immediately move to dismount, just tightened his hold on her. "You were a beautiful bride, *mo chridhe*. I cannae tell you how I felt, when you walked down the aisle toward me this morning and promised to be my wife."

She smiled at the memory. She'd felt like her heart had spent the day dancing. It had been a perfect wedding, with family and friends and everyone delighted for the bride and groom. Any ill feelings lingering from the scene in the library had faded to nothing over the last few weeks. Even Hamish and Diarmid had expressed their approval of the match, once they saw that Brody was deeply in love and set to stay that way.

Elspeth and her mother had reconciled soon after she accepted Brody's proposal. Today, Elspeth had been touched to see the redoubtable Lady Glen Lyon shed a tear when her daughter emerged from the vestry with her new husband to walk through the church as man and wife.

"You could try to tell me," she said, loving this ability to tease him.

In the days when she'd loved him from afar, she'd always felt utterly inadequate in comparison to superb Brody Girvan. Over this last month, they'd become equals. He was no longer the plaster god out of reach on his pedestal, and she was no longer the adoring acolyte, worshipping at his altar.

In fact, they'd managed to conquer the distance between them so effectively in the castle's hidden corners that she was astonished she'd come to church today as a virgin.

Brody was much more interesting and complex than the cipher she'd created in her imagination. A lifetime of discovering every facet of his nature stretched ahead of her. What she knew so far was warm and funny and passionate, with a streak of chivalry as wide as the Irish Sea. She looked forward to learning more about the passion tonight.

What a lucky girl she was.

"Och, I'd need to be a poet to do the moment justice." When she didn't speak to release him from the obligation, he sighed and kissed the top of her head. Even through the paisley shawl covering her hair, she felt the tenderness of his lips. "You're a demanding wench, Elspeth Girvan."

Her new name still thrilled her. She placed her gloved hands over his where they clasped her waist, holding her securely on the large horse. "You like that."

Their encounters since his proposal might have been frustrating, but they'd also proven educational. His unstinting need for her built her confidence that she was a desirable woman and even better, that the man she loved craved her to the point of madness.

"Aye, I do." He paused. "When you wed me, I thought I'd feel like I won a great victory."

"You didn't?"

"Aye. Aye, I did. But that wasn't the most important part."

"What was?"

"Mostly I felt thankful. And determined to do right by this treasure that life saw fit to grant to me. And love. Most of all, I felt love." His embrace tightened, and his voice lowered to the beautiful bass baritone that always made her shiver with longing. "I love ye, lassie. I'll love you until the day I die."

He paused, then went on with a fond impatience that coaxed a choked laugh from her. "Don't tell me you're crying again."

"How did you know?"

"I always know."

He did, she'd discovered. She sniffed. "You are a poet. That was lovely."

"Och," he said with charming bashfulness. "You're a daft wee thing."

"Daft with love," she said.

Brody slid down to the ground and raised his hands to pluck her from the saddle. He looked the complete dashing Highlander in his green and blue kilt. After the ceremony, he'd changed out of an elegant black coat that would grace any drawing room in London. Her wedding dress had been one of Sandra's creations, a simple gown in heavy silk the color of champagne. She'd also changed her clothing for the long ride up into the hills. Now she wore the rich purple riding habit that Marina and Fergus had given her as a wedding present.

As Brody set Elspeth down before him, she caught the glint of laughter in his green eyes. "Of course now what I mostly feel is randy. We have a wedding night ahead of us, and the Good Lord above knows why we're hanging around in a stable, when we could be inside doing wicked things to one another."

His earthy remarks made her laugh again, and she rose on her toes to kiss him. His lips were a delicious mixture of warmth and cold and tasted of winter air and Brody. "Don't take too long settling Perseus."

"Stay there. I'll be back soon."

"Stay here?"

"Aye. You'll see why."

In a radiant glow of anticipation, Elspeth watched him lead the horse into a stall. As he performed the humdrum actions of caring for his mount, she wrapped her arms around herself. She felt ready to explode with joy. Nobody in the history of the world had ever been as happy as she was right now.

Through the open door, she saw how the light faded on the wild hills and a starlit night crept in. A night that promised untold pleasures.

She and Brody would spend the next three days alone here at Achnasheen, before he took her to her new home at Invermackie. While she was eager to see the place he spoke of with such love, right now, she looked forward even more to changing from bride to wife. Hunger for her husband had risen to such a pitch, that she feared she'd burst into flame the instant he touched her.

"What are ye thinking about?" Brody crossed the floor toward her, his long legs eating up the space between them.

"You. Me. Us." Her blush burned in the cold air. "The fact that it's a long winter night, and we're going to spend it together."

His soft laugh expressed equal measures of anticipation and appreciation. "I have plans for each and every hour. Starting now."

He swung her into his arms. As her feet left the ground, her heart gave a great swoop. "Brody!"

"Whisht, *mo chridhe*. It's good luck to carry the bride over the threshold."

She curved one possessive hand around his neck. "Is it?"

He bent and kissed her quickly. "Och, it will be for us."

She murmured with disappointment when he drew away without deepening the kiss. Then she rested her head on his chest as he carried her across the short, snowy distance to the hunting lodge. Pushing the door open involved some delicious juggling of his burden, before he stepped inside.

"Goodness me, it's like something out of a dream," she said, as she took in the opulent room with its four-poster bed, comfortable furniture, and blazing fire. A quick, comprehensive glance confirmed that Fergus's retainers had fitted out the hunting lodge for the perfect honeymoon.

"Aye, it is. Fergus didn't let me come in, the day he brought me here to show me the path and to ask if I wanted to use the cottage for our first few nights together."

"Marina and Fergus have been very good to us."

"Aye, they have." Gently, Brody set her on her feet in front of the fire. "And I intend to be very good to you right now."

When she stared up into his bright green eyes, the purposeful light there made her shiver with yearning—and nerves. She loved him, she wanted him, he'd already put his hands on most of her body. But here in this luxurious retreat, she was powerfully aware that she'd never given herself to a man before.

"Do ye want to rest?" He tugged the Girvan tartan from over his shoulder and tossed it across a chair. He dropped onto one of the leather couches and with impressive dispatch, hauled off his boots.

Transfixed, Elspeth stood on the red and blue Turkey carpet in the center of the room and stared at him as he started to undress. Even his feet were beautiful. Strong and graceful and long.

"Elspeth?" he asked, humor deepening the attractive creases around his eyes.

She pressed one hand to where her heart performed a wild reel, and she shifted from foot to foot in a lather of impatience and agitation. "No."

He rose, fixing an unwavering regard on her that sent excitement rippling up and down her backbone. "Are ye hungry?"

"No," she said, although she hadn't done justice to the extravagant wedding breakfast that had emerged from the castle's kitchens.

"Do ye want some privacy?"

Humor tugged at her lips, as she removed her gloves. The gold glint of her wedding ring filled her with pride. "Do you want to go back out into the snow?"

He didn't smile. Over the last weeks, he'd leashed his hunger, but she saw that his control was coming to a rapid end. She gave another shiver.

"I suppose you're a wee bit nervous."

A soft huff of laughter escaped her. "Of course I'm nervous."

"So I thought—"

She stepped into the shelter of his body and placed her hands flat on his broad chest. Beneath her palm, his heart thundered as fast and hard as hers did. She sucked in a breath that tasted of Brody. Horses. Leather. The open air. Healthy male. A faint hint of musk that betrayed his desire.

"You're talking too much again, my love." She tugged his loose white shirt free of the thick black belt at his waist.

He caught her hands as she lifted the shirt. "Elspeth, lassie, are ye sure?"

A huff of disbelieving laughter escaped. "Brody, I've been sure for five years. I want you." She cast him a flirtatious glance under her eyelashes. "You've led me to believe you want me, too. Or have you deceived me, my handsome laddie?"

He laughed and wrenched his shirt from her hands and over his head. "Never let it be said."

She paused to appreciate the sight of his bare chest, hard and lean and covered with a scattering of silky black curls. With shaking hands, she unbuttoned her stylish jacket and, showing little respect for Sandra's skill and hard work, flung it across Brody's discarded plaid.

Brody fell to his knees before her. "Lift your foot."

Deftly he removed her halfboots, stockings and skirt, tossing them across the carpet. He caught her buttocks and dragged her forward, burying his face in her stomach. While she'd loved him for a long time, adult appetites were newer to her. Through all the feverish kisses and caresses of the last weeks, she thought she'd come to understand what it was to want a man. But only now when she stood in her undergarments in her husband's embrace did she really recognize the power of a woman's need.

"You're so beautiful," he groaned into the petticoats covering the soft curve of her belly.

Something loosened and liquefied deep inside her, and heat began to throb in the secret hollows of her body. She combed her fingers through his hair, as she quivered with an agonizing mixture of tenderness and desire for this man she'd married. The bed loomed behind them, the bed where he'd take her innocence before too much longer.

"I love you, Brody," she whispered and bent to kiss his ruffled dark crown. He tilted his head and met her lips. Kissing her all the time, he came to his feet. At first, gentleness was paramount, before passion inevitably took charge. A passion fed through a hundred fleeting encounters, where all that had kept her chaste was the chance of discovery.

With breathtaking competence, he removed the last of her clothing, sending corset, shift, petticoats and drawers drifting to the floor. Each brush of his hands on her skin stoked her restless longing for more.

"Oh, my," she sighed, even as she tried to cover her sex and her breasts.

He laughed with the fondness that had been among the first hints that his feelings were changing—that, and his penchant for kissing her whenever he had the chance. "Have I made ye shy?"

She blushed like fire and avoided those avid green eyes. "I'm sorry."

Brody stepped back, his hands loose at her waist, and surveyed her with a thoroughness that only intensified the warmth in her cheeks—and elsewhere.

"Don't be. It's charming." He laughed again. "Ye need bigger hands."

Ruefully she glanced down. She wasn't managing to hide much of her lavish bosom. That dratted shortbread. "Blast."

"Won't ye let me see you?" His brogue was thicker than ever, always a sign of overmastering emotion. "I've dreamed of having ye naked in my arms."

Elspeth raised uncertain eyes to meet his and found nothing but wonder and desire there. Thank goodness, he'd already made it clear he was mad about her abundant curves. "Have you?"

"Of course."

"These collywobbles must seem mad when you've touched me so often before."

As if he couldn't bear to look away, he went back to studying her bosom. "This is better."

On a couple of occasions after those shocking moments in the library, he'd fondled and kissed her breasts. She trembled to recall the thrill of his fingers playing with her nipples, nipples now tight and aching. Even the brush of her own hand across the hard peaks had her thinking sin.

"You look like you want to eat me," she said unsteadily, as the muscles at the base of her belly clenched on painful emptiness. How she wanted him.

"I've starved for you, Elspeth. You're lovely, and I adore you."

The words quietened the butterflies performing acrobatics in her stomach. Slowly she lifted her hands away from her body and straightened until she stood proudly before him.

Elspeth discovered how glorious it was, to have a man stare at her as if she were a goddess. A shaky inhalation expanded that imposing chest when he stepped back to see her better. Nerves fluttered back to life as his gaze devoured her nakedness, but she tilted her chin and made herself stand still as a statue.

"Take down your hair, my darling," he said hoarsely, his hands opening and closing at his sides.

As her clumsy fingers slid the pins from her hair, she watched his face. Her trepidation ebbed. While she saw flaring heat, she also saw raw need. Because of his worldly experience, Brody had always seemed ahead of her in this game. Tonight, their love for one another placed them on the same level.

As the waves of long, brown hair cascaded over her shoulders, it took no special act of courage for her to catch his hand and place it on her breast. "Touch me, Brody."

He groaned his assent, and in a flash, everything turned to pleasure and excitement. He caressed her breasts, squeezing and stroking, and taking the hard peaks of her nipples into his mouth. She cried out as sensation after sensation speared her, and the yearning ache between her legs sharpened to the edge of pain.

Astonishment faded, and she began her own journey of discovery, running her hands over the hot skin of his chest and shoulders and back. He pushed her backward with a few nudging steps, and she tumbled onto the bed, falling in a tangle of arms and legs and drifting hair.

"Make me yours, Brody." Dazed, enthralled, she stared up at him as he stood by the bed. "Don't make me wait any longer. I've already waited forever."

"Elspeth..." That proud, hawkish face softened so that if ever she'd doubted his love, she could never doubt it again. He stared at her as if she made the sun rise every day. Love shuddered through her. Love, and curiosity about how that love would find physical expression.

Her lips curved in a smile of welcome and to her amazement, the hand she extended toward him was steady. "Show me, my darling. Show me everything."

Brody's hands shook as he unbuckled his belt and unwrapped the kilt from around his waist. He was hard and heavy and ready for his wife. He watched Elspeth's eyes grow so large that they threatened to swallow him altogether.

His lips twitched. "Och, say something, lassie, or I'll think I've terrified ye into silence."

Her gaze still focused on the thick column of flesh rising between his thighs. She licked her lips with an unconscious sensuality that sent arousal thundering through him.

"My goodness me." Her gaze flickered up to meet his, then returned to his cock. "Will you fit?"

He laughed in delight and kneeled over her on the bed. "Aye, *mo chridhe*. With a bit of skill and a lot of care, I will indeed fit."

"I hope you're right," she said doubtfully, even as she buried her hands in his hair and brought him down for an urgent kiss that set his heart pumping.

Through the heat igniting his blood to fire, Brody remained aware that he was a large man, and his bride was a small woman, and a virgin besides. He was proud to be the first man to possess her, but he owed it to Elspeth to see that her first experience of a man was everything she hoped for.

While his mouth was demanding on hers, his touch retained a hint of gentleness as he explored the hills and valleys of her luscious body. By the time he stroked between her legs, she was quaking and gasping. Feminine arousal weighted the air with evocative perfume.

She was wet and slick under his fingers, and when he touched the center of her pleasure, she released a husky moan of encouragement. He took his time, although holding back nearly killed him. His balls were tight and heavy, and every beat of his heart shouted for him to take her.

He used his fingers to penetrate her and introduce her to the rhythm of love. She tightened, and her hands dug into his biceps. Her lovely face was flushed, her eyes turned black with desire, and her small white teeth sank into her full lower lip.

"Please..." she said in a strained voice. "Please, Brody. Don't torture me anymore."

"I dinnae want to hurt ye," he grated out, scraping his teeth down her neck, as she pulsed around the fingers he'd pushed inside her.

"It hurts me to want you this much. Don't make me beg."

Elspeth sounded on the verge of tears. He wasn't proof against her distress. Almost roughly, he parted her legs and shifted until he lay cradled between her thighs. He kissed her once more with every ounce of love he felt, before tenderness sank beneath his overwhelming need to claim her as his wife.

He pulled her knees up, hoping that might make what was to come easier for her. Then he tensed his hips, pulled back a fraction, and pushed forward with a steady ruthlessness that belied the storm of turbulent emotion in his heart.

She whimpered and went rigid under his invasion. By God, she was tight. He pressed onward, and felt her sharp flinch as he claimed her virginity. She didn't cry out, but her shaky moan made him wince. The need to thrust into her was a pounding drum behind his eyes, but he made himself proceed slowly and carefully.

"Breathe, Elspeth," he said on a broken gasp. He rose on his elbows to look at her. The creamy skin clung to the bones of her face, and her lips were thin with discomfort.

"If you think it will help," she said in a constricted voice.

"I do."

She closed her eyes and released a breath, before she snatched another. Her muscles eased around him, drawing him further inside her. With an incoherent murmur, she shifted and tilted her hips up. The change in angle seared him like lightning.

"It will get better," he said, dipping his head to kiss her.

After a hesitation that made his heart cramp, she kissed him back. "It's not too bad," she muttered against his lips.

"Wee liar," he said and kissed her again, longer this time. Her deathly grip on his arms softened, turned into a caress. With a sigh, she shut her eyes, and he felt her body loosen. He slid forward until she'd taken his full length.

Satisfaction flooded him, satisfaction and an ineffable sensation of homecoming. Possessing Elspeth was new and exciting and fresh, but it also felt like an act ordained from the beginning of time. When she squirmed with luxuriant enjoyment, he settled more snugly. She opened eyes alight with pleasure and love.

"You're right." She stroked the back of his neck with a gentle fervor that raged through him like wildfire. "It does get better."

"I told ye." He buried his head in her shoulder, feeling her body adjust to his. She clenched around him tighter than a fist. The connection extended beyond two bodies joined in a bed to something transcendent he'd never known before. That was love's alchemy, he supposed.

"There's more," he said and proved it by slowly pulling back, relishing how she clung to each inch.

"Oh, Brody..." she said in wonder. "I like that."

He laughed, despite his raging desperation, and slid into her again, the movement easier this time. Again he found that unforgettable welcome.

Elspeth wriggled once more, sparking a fierce hunger that he'd leashed until now, for the sake of her innocence. He could hold back no longer. On a guttural groan, he began to move in purposeful strokes that pushed her deep into the mattress. The rough saw of her breath was like music, as he struggled to last until she achieved her peak.

With every second, his control became more ragged. Through the blood roaring in his ears, he heard her give a sharp cry of ecstasy, and her body gripped him hard in a throbbing culmination.

As she tumbled over the edge, he thrust hard and felt his seed gush out of him. For a long time, he wandered lost in pulsating darkness and incomparable carnal pleasure. The power of his release blinded him, left him shaking and exhausted. And whole in a way he could never remember feeling before.

In giving himself so completely to Elspeth, he'd gained a new life.

Brody slumped onto his wife, overcome with the glory of what they'd just shared. He sucked in a fractured breath, tinged with the scent of sexual satisfaction.

"I love you, Elspeth," he whispered into the side of her neck. His world would never be the same.

Her arms curled around his back. "And I love you."

Without releasing her, he rolled to the side so he didn't crush his exquisite, passionate, naked bride. He smiled into her warm, damp skin. The simple, profound exchange of vows was the perfect ending to that sublime union.

Brody's embrace tightened. Elspeth was his, now and forever. Soon he and this wondrous lassie would go home to Invermackie, where a life of joy and purpose extended before them like a long, golden road. Each day, love would guide their steps into a shining future. He could hardly wait.

This year's Christmas at Achnasheen had brought him a gift beyond compare. And as any canny Scotsman knew, treasures were meant for cherishing. In the interest of further cherishing, he drew his bonny bride close into his body and kissed her until neither of them could see straight.

# ABOUT THE AUTHOR

Australian Anna Campbell has written 11 multi award-winning historical romances for Avon HarperCollins and Grand Central Publishing. As an independently published author, she's released more than 30 bestselling stories. Right now, she is working on a new series called A Scandal in Mayfair, set amidst the glamour and sensuality of Regency London. Anna has won numerous awards for her stories, including RT Book Reviews Reviewers Choice, the Booksellers Best, the Golden Quill (three times), the Heart of Excellence (twice), the Write Touch, the Aspen Gold (twice), and the Australian Romance Readers' favorite historical romance (five times).

Anna loves to hear from her readers. You can find her at:

Website: www.annacampbell.com

facebook.com/AnnaCampbellFans

twitter.comAnnaCampbellOz

bookbub.com/authors/anna-campbell

fame far and wide. When a carriage accident strands her at Achnasheen for a few weeks, it's a mixed blessing. The magnificent landscape offers everything her artistic soul could desire. If only she can resist the impulse to smash her easel across the laird's obstinate head.

***When two fiery souls come together, a conflagration flares.***

Marina is Fergus's worst nightmare—a woman who defies a man's guidance. Fergus challenges everything Marina believes about a woman's right to choose her path. No two people could be less suited. But when irresistible passion enters the equation, good sense soon jumps into the loch.

***Will the desire between Fergus and Marina blaze hot, then fade to ashes? Or will the imperious laird and his willful lass discover that their differences aren't insurmountable after all, but the spice that will flavor a lifetime of happiness?***

# The Laird's Christmas Kiss:
# The Lairds Most Likely Book 2

### *Down with love!*

Ever since she was fifteen, shy wallflower Elspeth
Douglas has pined in vain for the attentions of
dashing Brody Girvan, Laird of Invermackie. But
the rakish Highlander doesn't even know she's
alive. Now she's twenty, she realizes that she'll
never be happy until she stops loving her brother's
handsome friend. When family and friends gather
at Achnasheen Castle for Christmas, she intends to
show the world that she's all grown up, and grown
out of silly crushes on gorgeous Scotsmen. So take
that, my gallant laddie!

### *Girls just want to have fun...*

Except it turns out that Brody isn't singing from the
same Christmas carol sheet. Elspeth decides she's

not interested in him anymore, just as he decides he's very interested indeed. In fact, now he looks more closely, his friend Hamish's sister is pretty and funny and forthright – and just the lassie to share his Highland estate. Convincing his little wren of his romantic intentions is difficult enough, even before she undergoes a makeover and becomes the belle of Achnasheen. For once in his life, dissolute Brody is burdened with honorable intentions, while the lady he pursues is set on flirtation with no strings attached.

### *Deck the halls with mistletoe!*

With interfering friends and a crate of imported mistletoe thrown into the mix, the stage is set for a house party rife with secrets, clandestine kisses, misunderstandings, heartache, scandal, and love triumphant.

# The Highlander's Lost Lady:
## The Lairds Most Likely Book 3

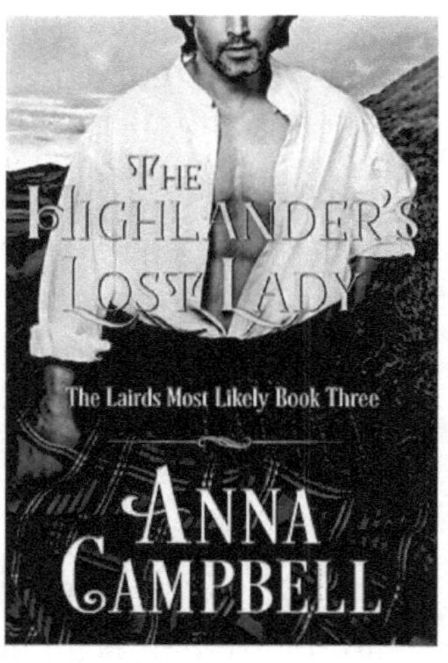

*A Highlander as brave and strong as a knight of old...*

When Diarmid Mactavish, Laird of Invertavey, discovers a mysterious woman washed up on his land after a wild storm, he takes her in and tries to find her family. But even as forbidden dreams of sensual fulfillment torment him, he's convinced that this beautiful lassie isn't what she seems. And if there's one thing Diarmid despises, it's a liar.

*A mother willing to do anything to save her daughter...*

Widow Fiona Grant has risked everything to break free of her clan and rescue her adolescent daughter from a forced marriage. But before her quest has barely begun, disaster strikes. She escapes her brutish kinsmen, only to be shipwrecked on Mactavish territory where she falls into her enemies' hands. For centuries, a murderous feud has raged between the Mactavishes and the Grants, so how can she trust her darkly handsome host?

*Now a twisted Highland road leads to danger and passion...and irresistible love. But is love strong enough to banish the past's long shadows and offer these wary allies all that their hearts desire?*

***Peace in the glens means war in the bedchamber!***

Scotland. 1699. In a time of heroes, the greatest hero of all is Callum Mackinnon, Laird of Achnasheen. Brave, reckless, canny, and handsome enough to turn any lassie weak at the knees, Callum is a legend in the wild corner of the Highlands where he rules. Now the young laird is determined to choose a new path for his clan and end the violent feud with the Drummonds, a conflict that has painted the glens red with blood for centuries. This means taking Bonny Mhairi Drummond, the Rose of Bruard, as his wife. When negotiations with her pig-headed father break down, Callum seizes matters into his own hands and kidnaps the fairest maiden in Scotland, swearing to make her his own.

Bonny Mhairi is the adored only child of Clan

Drummond's doughty chieftain and she's inherited all her father's courage and stubbornness. Not to mention his undying hatred for anyone called Mackinnon. When the Mackinnon chieftain steals her away from her home and vows to woo her into accepting him as her husband, she swears that she'll never consent to be his bride. But trapped inside her foe's castle, Mhairi finds it hard to cling to old certainties. She detests her arrogant jailer, even as he sparks a fierce, forbidden hunger in her soul.

**_Loving the enemy..._**

As Callum and Mhairi wage their passionate war of hearts, danger, treachery and desire circle closer and closer. When her father's army masses at the gates of Achnasheen, will Mhairi prove herself a Drummond now and forever? Or will new allegiances trump ancient hatred, as the desperate laird battles to win the lass he loves more than his life?

# The Highlander's Christmas Quest:
# The Lairds Most Likely Book 5

*She's found the man for her, but he has no plans to stay on her island. Perhaps it's time to try a little sabotage!*

Scotland. 1725. The moment she sees handsome Dougal Drummond, Kirsty Macbain tumbles headlong into love. A chance storm a few days before Christmas has blown the gallant Highlander off-course to her father's isle of Askaval, but once he's repaired his boat, Dougal is determined to continue on his way. His bright blue eyes are firmly fixed on valiant deeds and a distant horizon. What does he care for a smart-mouthed, independent lassie who forms no part of his plans for his future?

Kirsty is convinced that if only she can keep Dougal on Askaval, he'll see how perfect they are together. With his boat out of action, he's trapped in her company. Some surreptitious midnight destruction with a drill and a hammer might help true love to win out. On the other hand, if Dougal discovers what she's been up to, there will be the devil to pay.

Will this madcap Christmas deliver Kirsty's heart's desire – or will her scheming see Dougal sailing away to a life without her?

# The Highlander's English Bride:
## The Lairds Most Likely Book 6

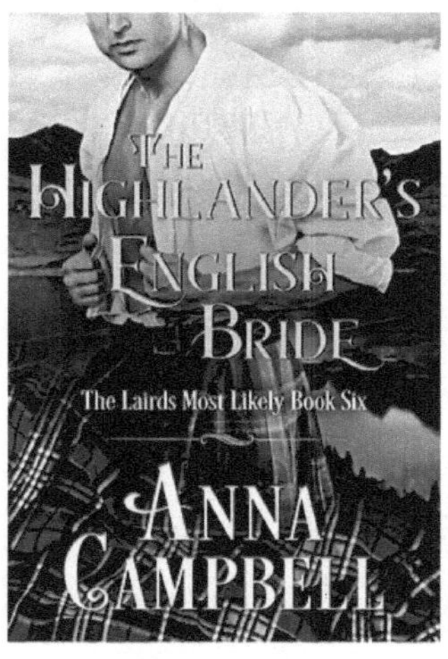

*An impossible pairing...*

Hamish Douglas, the mercurial Laird of Glen Lyon,
has never got along with independent, smart-
mouthed Emily Baylor. Which wouldn't matter if
this brilliant Scottish astronomer didn't move in the
same scientific circles as Emily and if her famous
father wasn't his mentor. But when Emily looks
likely to derail the event which will make Hamish's
career, he loses his temper with the pretty miss and
his recklessness leaves her reputation in ruins.

*A marriage made in scandal...*

Emily has always thought her father's spectacular
protégé was far too arrogant for his own good. But
what is she to do when the only way she can save
her good name in society is to wed the unruly laird?
Reluctantly she accepts Hamish's proposal, but

only on the condition that their union remains
chaste. That shouldn't be a problem; they've never
been friends, let alone potential lovers – except that
after they marry, Hamish reveals unexpected
depths and a host of admirable qualities, and he's
so awfully handsome, and now the swaggering
rogue admits that he desires her...

*From the ballrooms of London to the
grandeur of the western Highlands, a battle
royal rages between these two strong-
willed combatants. Neither plans to yield
an inch – but are these smart people smart
enough to see that sometimes the greatest
victory lies in mutual surrender?*

# The Highlander's Forbidden Mistress: The Lairds Most Likely Book 7

***A week to be wicked...***

Widowed Selina Martin faces another marriage founded on duty, not love. When notorious libertine Lord Bruard invites her to his isolated hunting lodge, he promises discretion – and seven days of hedonistic pleasure before she weds her boorish fiancé. All her life, Selina has done the right thing, but this no-strings-attached chance to discover the handsome rake's sensual secrets is irresistible. She'll surrender to her wicked fantasies, seize some brief happiness, then knuckle down to a loveless union. What could possibly go wrong?

In a lifetime of seduction, Brock Drummond, the dashing Earl of Bruard, has never wanted a woman the way he wants demure widow Selina Martin. When Selina agrees to become his temporary lover, he soon falls captive to an enchantment unlike any other. He sets out to slake his white hot desire until only ashes remain, but as each day of forbidden delight passes, the idea of saying goodbye to his ardent mistress becomes more and more unbearable.

When scandal explodes around them and threatens to destroy Selina, Brock is the only person she can turn to. After so short a time, can she trust a man whose name is a byword for depravity?

***Will this sizzling liaison prove a mere affair to remember? Or will their week of passion spark a lifetime of happiness for the widow and her dissolute Scottish earl?***

# The Highlander's Christmas Countess: The Lairds Most Likely Book 8

***The new stableboy has a secret!***

Kit Laing is a genius with Glen Lyon's horses and a favorite with his employer's family, but he isn't all he seems. In fact, the shy stablehand isn't a he at all. Kit is actually Christabel Urquhart, Countess of Appin, on the run from a greedy, violent stepbrother with designs on her fortune.

***And the laird's handsome nephew has worked out just what it is.***

Quentin MacNab, the dashing heir to Cannich, has had his suspicions about the new stable lad from the first. Kit is far too pretty to be a boy – and far too well spoken to be a servant.

*Now passion and danger combine to create a Yuletide like no other.*

When a snowstorm traps Kit and Quentin overnight in an isolated hut, the discovery of her true identity sparks a rushed marriage to stave off a scandal. But can the Christmas Countess learn to trust her charming new husband's promises of protection? Or will their fragile alliance fall victim to the evil forces assailing her?

# The Highlander's Rescued Maiden: The Lairds Most Likely Book 9

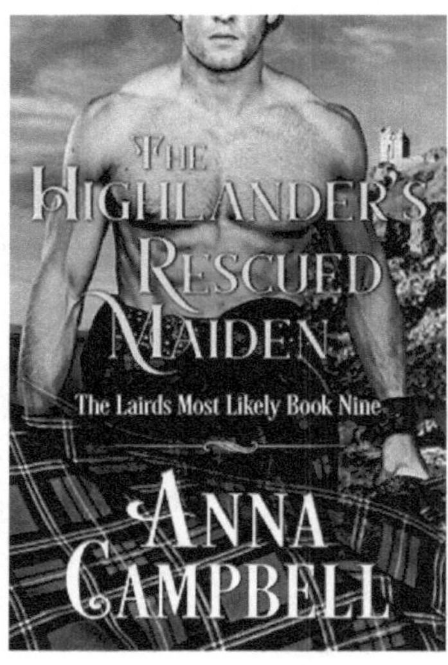

*The myth of Fair Ellen of the Isles.*

Across the Highlands, people recount the legend of a beautiful lassie in a tower, locked away from her clamorous suitors by a tyrannical father. Any person of sense dismisses the story as a fairy tale, no more substantial than a wisp of Scottish mist.

*Rogue or hero? Or a little bit of both?*

Dashing Highlander Will Mackinnon is a devil with the ladies, disinclined to fall for such romantic nonsense. But one day, his storm-tossed boat washes ashore at a rocky island dominated by a stone tower. Inside the tower, he discovers lovely, gallant Ellen Cameron and a passion that eclipses anything he's experienced before in his reckless life.

*Danger and desire...*

This brave adventurer vows to rescue the captive maiden and make her his own forever. But dark shadows gather about the lovers and threaten to destroy all their hopes for happiness. Will has found the love of a lifetime – but will it end up costing him his life?

# The Highlander's Christmas Lassie:
## The Lairds Most Likely Book 10

***Young love torn apart.***

As teenagers, Malcolm Innes and Rhona Macleod
fell passionately in love. But Malcom's parents were
horrified to think of the aristocratic heir to Dun
Carron marrying a humble crofter's daughter.
Desperate to crush the affair, they locked Malcolm
up and exiled Rhona to London where she
disappears. But Malcolm is faithful and stubborn
and devotes his life to searching for his beloved and
the child she was carrying when they were cruelly
separated.

***A chance to mend two shattered lives.***

On a snowy Christmas Eve, Rhona opens the door
of her isolated farmhouse to find the man she never

thought to see again, the man who betrayed her. When she was pregnant with his son, Malcolm abandoned her to find her way alone in a cold, heartless world. Now she discovers that her long-held hatred is based on lies and that he's been true to her. Yet surely after all these years, it's too late to awaken the love that once united them.

*As Christmas Eve turns into Christmas Day, Malcolm and Rhona discover that their mutual desire has never died. Will this Yuletide reunion lead to a lifetime together? Or has old tragedy ruptured their bond forever?*